Where the sky meets the earth

It's just beyond there

The
Horizon
Tree

NEIL STANNERS

Published by Garamonde 2023

GARAMONDE

ISBN 978-1-86275-017-3

Production by Media Services
Cover photo - Neil Stanners

Neil Stanners was born in Sydney.

He lived and worked in Europe.

He now resides once again in Sydney.

CONTENTS

THE HORIZON TREE

It's the only one.

Well, I couldn't see it.

Now there's a conflicting mix taking place in my body.

There's fear, hopelessness, loneliness and hunger and

thirst. All within minutes of the assessment of my

situation. From carefree and curious to dismay.

The land was one and the one was empty. It lay about to

all points from my position. Just flat, without feature or

form.

A great sea of nothing. Soft and blurred at the edges by

heat haze.

Had I have been of a disposition, to drop to my knees, to

take time and be of fair mind, I dare say there were many
features. Small particles of interest, even life, adapted to
this mix of reddish soil, flattened scrub, harsh light and a
vast ongoing repetitive same.

On a human scale, my mind was elsewhere. Peril stalked
my place on the ground.

I am not a man of the outdoors. Gentle walks through
parks among trees and grass with a lake or stream close
by does not harden or prepare you for a wilderness that
has none of the aforementioned niceties. City people
should adjust slowly and use a degree of caution, of
respect for their relocated neighborhood.

I felt I had. This trip was not taken within weeks of arrival.
I was acclimatised, settled in, almost a part of the
town. Local people knew me. First names were used
in conversations. Now I understood. The town had
boundaries and I had unwittingly stepped over the border.
I was quite surprised at the degree of calamity that swiftly
overtook me once I became aware of my new situation.

My vehicle did not wish to continue. It lacked fuel and the
will, borne out by strange new noises of protest. With half
a bottle of warm water some digestive biscuits and one
apple, I could see the range of judgment errors I had made
when I undertook this journey. A journey based on a talk
to a man who knew of a place via several conversations

previous that may be what I was seeking.

A simple request, a simple plan, a simple undertaking.

Not so, it seemed.

It is the nature of the first nation people to be stoic and clever with their land however their concepts of time, distance and geographical reference can best be described as vague. So the information passed to me by a white man may have been sullied without him being aware of its faults. Was I unwise to trust him? Perhaps he knew that I was not all that clever with this country and its ability to grab you.

Despite my awareness of these idiosyncrasies and their possible consequences I had decided quite hastily to pack a few items and follow the directions told to me in a tin-framed miner's claim work-office while sipping odd scotch whiskey. The best low cost compromise I could find in the hotel shop.

He even drew me a map. This white man who knew a few of the desert people. To a place he had never been so he said. On it, my current position was marked down as 'small flat area'.

The whole distance was estimated to be a 'little' over 30 kilometres yet I had exhausted, it seemed, 50 kilometres just to reach the 'flat area' described on his map. An area of daunting vastness. Was it even the right 'area'? There were no roads after the first 10 kilometres only a compass bearing based on the sun's position, the time of year and the note. My direction may not have always been exact. A straight line as it were.

It was one of the cooler months. A relative term based on its relation to the intensely hot months of the summer. It seems even the original people of this land knew there was no joy in making the journey except in spring and autumn.

The town had ample water from springs and creeks. Beyond the town the country dried out rapidly. What could induce people in a pleasant environment to head into a dusty unfriendly locale? What enjoyment could they seek or find?

Living in these towns, doing meaningless work, allows the mind to wander. Familiar with the local inhabitants and relaxed in their company, the land becomes part of your psyche. You accept it. It holds no command of your fears. Life and time become a vague minor opera, strutting along to a distant conclusion that the players are uninterested in reaching or even acting out. It all just happens. The next day, the same act with slight variations.

Observations of day to day events become part of the process of living in communities where very little happens apart from what always happens. The routine is the norm. A slight change is therefore easy to note.

I noticed it the second year. Mentioned it casually to Alice in the little food market in Peculiar Street.

"Where have all the Natives gone?"

The natives were the first nation people who carried out various jobs in the town. If you were white or Asian or some other race you didn't qualify. They were quite proud of their many thousands of years head start in the land. Nobody else could be a native. Although the natives of this town were 'different'. When I first arrived I assumed there were none. To a person making a brief survey, they would be nearly indistinguishable from the rest of the town population. I could guess, not ask, the reason.

A great deal of racial mixing had perhaps occurred.

"Usual place," she replied, as if answering a question that did not need to be asked.

She paused. Stopped packing my food into my carry bag and added, "You're a newbie. I forgot." Then she proceeded to put away my purchases.

"And ..... ?"

"Well, they head off ..... to a place they like, somewhere out there."

She waved a can of my beans in the general direction of the door and the outskirts of town.

"Left this morning. They reappear a bit later. One day they're just back, workin' or doing their thing. Running their businesses. As if it was all a dream."

I handed over my money.

"Fascinating stuff."

Alice brushed some hair from her face then took my notes.

"Don't bother asking where they go. They won't tell you. It's not knowledge they want to share."

She stopped and gave an odd little smile.

"I think a couple of the guys who have the mine leases out on the south hill might know something. They're pretty close to some of the younger ones that work there. Personally, I'm all for it. Wherever they go they come back happy and never cause problems. Seem revitalized. Must be a good place with lots of things to do We've got a good relationship with the first nation people. Unique you might say."

"Well after all they're just fellow humans," I said lightheartedly.

She stopped, looked at me for a moment. Made a little sound.

"No, they're not. They live elsewhere. It's another place. Might look the same to us but what they see is not what we see."

"That's profound."

"You can laugh. It all makes sense once you know."

Here I must point out that in hindsight I now know I was

being played with like a cat with a mouse. Alice and the others were good at that.

I had, first of all, concluded that all those who disappeared were of aboriginal descent. As I noted, it was hard to recognise racial lines in this town. Secondly, Alice was not a casual confidante joining me in some idle gossip.
Thirdly, my inquiries were crafted and encouraged to produce a degree of curiosity that would cause me to follow a cleverly constructed path along which I was being guided.
The wilderness, the terror, was part of the plan. Training, testing, amusement I never discovered the motivation.

This bi-annual phenomenon passed from my interest for a short while. About a month to put a time on it. As I went out one mid-morning, to post some mail, I saw two of them standing on the corner deep in conversation.
They were back!
These two took orders and waited on tables in the Majestic Cafe just around the corner. The cafe was a large ornate establishment that defied its location by looking European and producing quite a sophisticated and varying menu. The chef was a largely silent man who worked with two talented native assistants and

experimented constantly. The cuisine was French.
The waiters were refined, pleasant and efficient and knew
some things about food that often surprised me. My stare
elicited a friendly acknowledgment in the form of a head
nod.

"You're back. Good to see you. Will the Majestic menu be
even better? I mean now you're in charge again?"

"That's not for us to judge, sir. You call in and give us your
opinion, eh. I just bring out the food."

He grinned.

I was now facing them. They were quite smartly dressed
in their standard white shirts, black pants and dark
green aprons. Their whole manner and dress was quite
European. Like a couple of exotic staff having a break on
the Boul'Mich.

"I suspect there's more to it. There always is with your
place. I'll be there for lunch. Anything you recommend?"

The younger one whose name badge is, Phillipe, nodded
with a slight grin.

"Flight came this morning with fresh perch. When you're
this far from the coast the day to eat fish is the day it
arrives, eh. We gave the chef some finger limes and some
other stuff we brought back. Bit of butter, cream, a few
other things. It'll taste pretty special."

A drop of silence ensued.

"Back from where?"

"What do you mean?"

"Where have you come back from?"

"From the bush. Out there."

The young man waved in general direction over his shoulder.

"Yes, but where exactly do you fellas all go? It's more desert, scrub plains. No bush is there?"

Their look was hard to read. As if dealing with a child asking questions beyond their ken.

"You know we can't tell you that."

"Why not?"

The older one, who might have been a brother leaned a little closer. He screwed up his face just slightly and smiled.

"Because it's a secret," he whispered.

I tried to look hurt.

"So you don't trust us white guys?"

"No, of course we don't. Although some whities are part of it aren't they."

I paused then took a turn at leaning closer. These riddles were always the same.

"So there's whities involved? You allow your trusted secret to cross over to the enemy."

"Hey, you not the enemy, Mister. You're a nice guy. Lot of respect for you. Same with these other fellas. Special whities. These special ones, they're okay."

"Who are these 'other fellas'?"

"We can't tell you that, it's a secret."

I laughed. I couldn't help it.

They also seemed to be enjoying the cut and thrust of this pointless conversation.

"I may try to find out."

My statement did not cause a ripple. It was apparently beyond even consideration.

"You want me to have the chef put some fish aside for you?" said Joshua, according to his name tag.

I had been dismissed.

"Yes, yes that would be good."

"12.30 okay?"

"Yes. 12.30. Thanks." I continued to the post office.

The fish was magnificent. Filleted, pan-fried with subtle spicy lime pepper flavours. Whatever they did in that cafe it was unique and hard to understand.

The next day I rang Main du Destin Mine Co. After considering the situation it seemed they would be the most likely. They were a mid-sized local business. There was a big mining outfit as well. One that had a lot of foreign money in it. But apparently, they were struggling to find any useable mineral deposits. Word was they would eventually close and be gone within a

month. I suspected that the townsfolk had engineered their downfall. The others were small locally manned operations. The word about was that Main du Destin and the others were doing very well. My understanding of mining and minerals was rudimentary. I was not even sure what they mined. My job did not involve such areas.
I reported only on areas of knowledge as per my contract.

He said, "Yes," he would see me. Surprise. I was expecting rejection. Though my reasons for asking to speak with him were vague, so it could still go awry.
As I drove up to their entrance I questioned why I wanted to know the story anyway. Not my business, not my town. Was it simply boredom? A small quest away from the routine of my work.

He smiled and leaned back in his chair. We sipped tumblers of whiskey from the bottle I had offered as a bribe or token.
"Why are you interested?"
"It's boredom and curiosity. Small town. I've little to do and there's this oddity that occurs a number of times a year."
He waited.
"I don't understand why. I believe that some town white people are involved."

There, I'd admitted my reasons in the first sentence.
Might as well keep going.

"All the first nation people disappear. I know, I know.
It's their nature, to go wandering off periodically but
not a whole lot together, not overnight and not in
such an organised and mysterious way. They're not
unsophisticated types, living in a town camp. In Ville
Perdu, they're smart, clever, with talents and businesses.
They have something extra. They're hardly recognisable.
So, I want to know what is happening."

"And you think I can help? Why?"

"From the little I could extract from people in town, you
have a special relationship with these people. You employ
quite a few and they 'get along' with you. You know
things."

The mining man sat forward.

"You're a bit misinformed it would seem. Townspeople
making mischief. Too many assumptions. I've heard you
do an excellent job in town. Your work seems to be in
the best interest of all the people here. You're efficient,
courteous, friendly and well-liked. After a couple of
years, you might consider yourself a local but you're not.
That takes generations. So, considering you're actually a
newcomer I don't like your tone. Some in the past have
been mildly curious. You're the first to be blatantly nosy."

My direct approach was crumbling as I sat in his little
office. He was a muscular man with his blue-sleeved shirt
rolled up high on his arms. A miner, not an intellectual? Or
a miner and an intellectual? I was to be shown the door?
Then it all changed. He smiled and then chuckled.

"Did you enjoy the fish?"

"Pardon?"

"Phillipe, the waiter you spoke to, said you liked the fish
he told you about."

"How?"

"Small town. These people talk to me. It's a trust thing.
I passed whatever test may have taken place. Been chosen
for no reason. But they're wise, they share some things.
All part of the knowledge. So I accept my role whatever it
is and carry on."

He paused and sipped his whiskey.

"I've tasted better and I've tasted worse. But I appreciate
your gesture. Just don't talk to the town whities. Silly
gossip."

"But you're a white."

"Yes, I know, 'chosen'."

"Do you know where they go?"

"Yes."

"Have you ever been?"

"It's for them, not for us."

"So, yes? Where? What happens?"

"You know I can't tell you that. Even if I have been."

"Then I'm back at the brick wall I keep running into."

"No, you're not. You can go."

"Pardon?"

"You can go. Nothing stopping you."

"I can?"

"Yes. You're a man who coordinates local health. We like you. So, at least I can point you in a particular direction. You'll get in maybe or be told to go away. There's no way of knowing. If you're that interested it's a chance you can take. Find out for yourself. I'll draw you a map. Would that make you happy?"

He did draw me a map. Asked if I could use a compass. I said yes.
Then he suggested I never make inquiries.
"When you notice they've gone, you get going and head off as fast as you can. Won't be till sometime in Spring now so you've got some time to relax."

I shook his hand, insisted he keep the whiskey and turned to the door. He added something.
"I want you to know about this lot. You're a newbie so I can tell you. You're right. They're different. No town camps, no drunks. All neat, clean, tidy, in jobs or businesses and quite worldly. Other towns have problems,

we don't. Why is that do you suppose? What is it about this town? Once I arrived here I knew I was in the right place. Where I should be. The one thing they won't tell me is what tribe they're from. That's mysterious isn't it?"

"I thought the tribal connection was something important."

"It probably is, just different. It's like they're aliens. Influenced by different forces."

"You sound a bit like Alice. You know Alice, she's at the market .... "

"I know Alice. She told me you might turn up here someday."

As I departed I added.

"You have a French name. How does a Frenchman finish up running a mine in a strange little town in an empty place like Australia?"

He looked at me for some seconds. I had the impression he was about to say something then held back.

"History. It can create pathways you would not normally take. Then fate decides you will."

It was another riddle. I wanted to pursue it but I was already being ushered out the door and away.

Oh, the fun they were having with me.

The remains of winter passed by a day at a time. Some mornings were hard. Motivation was an essence I sought but rarely found. I had two more years of a five-year contract to see out. Why I had accepted the deal was perplexing. A love affair over and a chance to save a lot of money. The latter only partly realised because alcohol is quite expensive out here.

At dinner, on a day like all the others, in the Majestic Cafe, Phillipe presented himself at my table. He smiled and tilted his head in a knowing fashion.

"What would like today, sir."

"Please don't call me 'sir'."

"We have to, it's polite."

"How long have I been coming here? I hardly know you, Phillipe. But surely enough to use first names."

He ignored my suggestion. In the brief silence that hung in the air, I tried a different approach.

"I see you always have a cassoulet on the menu. There's quite a lot of French cuisine. Was the chef trained in France?"

This seemed to amuse Phillipe, although he contained his facial movement to a brief flicker.

"You are right of course, sir. There does seem to be a bias toward French influences however we're always seeking to combine local bush produce and invent unique dishes and unusual flavours. Today the chef's done some spicy meat dumplings. He says he invented them. He calls them 'Migaloo Packets'. I tried one. Damn nice."

"Are you married?"

Phillipe was startled but he answered.

"Yes. Married young."

"Children?"

"Boy ten. Girl nine."

"Are you happy?"

Phillipe had reached his mysterious limits.

"I'll put you down for two Migaloo Packets. They're big. Still, once you taste the first you gonna want a second."

He wandered off. Cut short but I felt I had made progress.

The Migaloo Packets were beef and kangaroo mixture in a soft pastry. A sort of dumpling. Oddly spiced by potions I did not recognise. They had a strange salty, smoky sweetness, unlike anything I'd experienced.

They were delicious. I definitely wanted the second. The Majestic mystery continued. After nearly an entire bottle of Shiraz, I made my way back to my large upstairs flat over the delicatessen and slept till after ten the next morning.

It happened in early spring. Rarely, I decided to head to the Majestic for breakfast. Hard week. Bit of a treat.

As I entered, the barman pointed to a note pinned to his counter.

OUR GARCONS ARE AWAY FOR A WHILE.

GIVE ME YOUR ORDERS AND I'LL PASS THEM
TO THE KITCHEN.
COLLECT YOUR ORDERS HERE.

I closed off my work mid-morning. Grabbed the map, some spare clothes, bottle of water. That should do it.

I'd be there in a few hours.

By nightfall I was desperate. On a road, there is at least the chance of a vehicle making its way past. I was a speck in a huge empty landscape. No roads went anywhere near this place.

In my mind, I could see the aerial view. It was bleak.

My car was so tiny in the vast nothingness about me.

I slept fitfully through the night, cramped and miserable on the car's back seat.

By 9.00 am the heat of the day drove me out of my vehicle. Despite sipping and managing my water it was now all gone.

One indelible fact hung in my brain. Do not leave your vehicle. People who wander off, thinking they can make it to some road, contact point or help invariably end their days alone and dead.

I banged my head in frustration, at my impulsive, stupid act. What made me think of doing this in a land that is so completely unforgiving? A land where people disappear. Set up by a man in mining.

Did he find my little quest amusing? If I did locate where

they went they'd chase me away.

I was trespassing at best on a culture that did not welcome intrusion.

"Look for the Horizon Tree," he'd said. "You'll know it."

God, I was so thirsty. The sun became a glaring brutal, all-encompassing beast that hunted me like a rabbit in headlights. Inside the car afforded shelter but was so hot, I would sweat away the remaining moisture in my body. Outside, even with a large piece of random cloth wrapped around my head and hanging down over my neck I was tortured and exposed, ripped by tentacles of relentless radiation.

I knelt down in a tiny shadow afforded me by the sun's position. Seated on the dirt I could just manage to lean against the car's heated bodywork. As I sat I idly ran my hands about in the soil and under the vehicle. It felt cooler. A temporary answer? Laying down I performed a snake-like shuffle across and into the dark underworld of the car. Centering myself I worked about until a hollow of reasonably cooler soil was formed under my body. I was now at a temperature that was bearable. For some inexplicable reason on this still merciless day, a slight breeze moved under the car in the shadow and lowered the heat of my sweat.

My world was now a view of the car differential and

exhaust pipes. There seemed to be a slight oil leak from around the motor area. A drip appeared on my leg. The car had no rust, despite its age. A small advantage of dry desert air. I was surprised at how clean my vehicle's underbelly appeared. My inspection lasted several minutes until my mind was drawn back to my perilous situation. Once again I focused on the world about me. To each side lay a bright slit of sunlit scrubby landscape framed by the car, the earth and the sets of tyres.
A small procession of disinterested ants wandered by. Some briefly gazed into the shade afforded by the car but chose to continue their journey in the bright sunlight.
I felt tired. So tired.
My last thoughts were, "This is where I am going to die."

How long I lay in pity and vague slumber I do not know. Many hours at least. A sound awoke me. For some seconds I stared at my exhaust system running close to my nose above my head. My mouth and throat were dry. Where was I? With a rush it came back. Had I heard a noise, perhaps a motor running or had I been dreaming of some miracle rescue?
Turning I looked out from my refuge. I blinked trying to focus, to comprehend. There seemed to be a small set of feet standing next to the vehicle. Then an inverted face appeared. A face that belonged to the feet. A face that

smiled encouragingly. A girl, perhaps nine."

"Hello, Mister, What you doin' down there?"

Another face appeared. A boy, about ten.

"Ahh", he said.

The faces disappeared and their voices called.

"Found him. He's under here."

Other voices answered. Other feet appeared. Some shoes and some boots. Somebody was in my car. They turned the key briefly, checking ignition. More talking then there was a clattering sound and a gurgle. Petrol was being poured into my tank.

Nobody had suggested I get out from my hole in the dirt. I looked again at the children's feet.

They were quite light coloured. The ongoing trait and mystery in the town's aboriginal residents. None were dark. More a Polynesian shade. No, even less. A liaison with light-skinned folk that must have been happening in the area for quite some time. I had pondered these same thoughts many times. Why was I laying under a car in the desert right now, examining the idea once more? It added to the whole strange atmosphere.

The next face to appear belonged to some boots. The man from Main du Destin Mining.

"Did I not mention that you should fuel up?"

He continued staring as if waiting for me to suggest the next move. He held out his hand.

"Well, come on, out of there. You're looking a little distressed. Phillipe can drive your car the rest of the way. Travel with me. We'll talk. Would you like a nice cold drink?"

It was so close as it happened. The 'flat area' was actually a subtle low area.

Should the man next to me have mentioned this trick of the landscape that would have confused me? Possibly he knew exactly what would happen.

After a few minutes of driving, the small truck revved and headed up a gentle slope. As it flopped over the grassy lip a range of very high, steep, hills or small mountains appeared as if pushed out of the ground by some theatrical stage mechanics. They had a softness to them. A blue filtered light outlined in the sun.

My driver rolled forward a little way and then stopped the vehicle.

"Do you see it now?"

"Pardon?"

"Run your eye along the top of the hills. Look carefully."

I did as he suggested. Then I smiled.

"Ahh. The horizon tree. It's not fake at all. That's something. It must have been a monster in its day."

"Yes, back when this was a lush green area. I suppose it just grew and reached for the sky. No idea how long it's been dead but the locals have it in their stories so quite a few hundred years. My guess is the dry atmosphere preserves it."

"And it became a symbol. To guide them to this place."

"Correct. If you'd had more petrol in your tank you should have travelled up to here and all of this would have been revealed."

I didn't mention that I had been preparing for death and that even with more fuel in my tank I would probably have still given up as I did..

My car slid to a halt next to the truck. Then two other vehicles full of the town's native population. Still more rolled up. Not all were native. There were many of the town's white population. Whole families. People I would not have expected or would have noticed were missing. Phillipe nodded and smiled from my car. His wife sat beside him. His two children in the back. All these people seemed the same to me now.

"You're noticing how many people are involved aren't you," said my driver. "Not everybody can go every time. Can't leave the town empty. Quite a while back they set a system of quarterly visits. A rest in between gave it all a chance to adjust. We decided not to come back the same day to keep life a little on the normal side."

I looked at the man as he spoke.

"You know all about this place. I understand none of it.

Especially those last words."

"Of course you don't. Not yet. Then, my friend, you will be surprised. So very surprised. We haven't had a newbie for some time. A lot is happening right now. They will watch you, to see your reaction."

"What was the conversation in your office about?"

"Oh, just banter. While we decided whether you should be included. It's a long process. Us original whities are a part of it. Unless you're somebody like Alice for instance. Then a decision has to be made about your future."

"So I passed your scrutiny?"

"You did."

"What if I'd failed?"

"Steps would have been taken."

The man's tone suggested no further information would be forthcoming.

"Is this the whole convoy?"

He glanced at the assembled lines of vehicles, counting and making a total.

"One more of our group to come."

We sat in silence for several hot, earth creaking minutes then I turned to my saviour.

"How did you leave before me and finish up behind me?" I asked.

"We camped last night. There's no rule about hurrying.

A few others have to come, from other directions. Most of
us are in Ville Perdu. "

At risk of annoyance, I repeated my line of questioning.
"You're in this. You knew all along. I sat in your office
and you gave me a vague message about the mysterious
people who you did not understand."

The owner of Main du Destin Mining Co. leaned back, as
was his way.

"I know," he said. "It's complicated. I had to ask. Make a
story. They had to decide. You're a guest but once you're
in there's no going back. Whatever happens next, keep
that in mind."

"What's an 'original whitie?" I asked.

The sound of another vehicle could be heard. A second
Main du Destin Mining truck made its way to the lineup
and braked, its motor rumbling.

"Alice is a slow but methodical driver." He smiled.

"Are those canoes on top of that truck?"

"Yes, they are."

It is my story. I am one of few 'newwhiteys' to be allowed
past the tree. Why you are chosen is not asked or
explained. They liked me it seemed from the moment I
arrived in the town because I looked so miserable and lost
all the time but was still respectful. The precise process

is unfathomable. I think it's akin to picking up stray souls. And this explanation was given to me third hand, so it suits the narrative. The initial visit was all prearranged anyhow. These things are not allowed to just 'happen'. Some amusement and observations at my expense. I understand now.

My department has accepted my request to stay on.
I doubt anybody else would have wanted my appointment out here.
The earth is a quite surprising place when you look.
It sometimes hides the most delightful and unexpected pieces of its jewellery collection and waits for the observant among us to find its little treasures. Certainly, I now believe there is much we have not found or even suspect could exist.

As we left that first time, I stopped at one stage and looked back. The tree had a purpose. Though it only marked the crossover point. Nothing definite. All cloaked in layers of protective uncertainty. From its base, beside its grey hard trunk, there was a vague way forward. The subtlety was natural and yet it has an air of planning about its structure.
For the curious with time and need to know it signalled, safe in the knowledge that few would come or have the

time, or wish to climb a little further, travel round a last outcrop of rock and look about, to see why it beckoned. This tree, so high and aloof on the horizon.

35

Of course, I can say no more. Please, don't ask. I am bound by trust. It is a secret.

THE TOURISTS

This town, where they finally stopped, after a lengthy, whole day of rolling along a strip of bitumen that rose and fell and never seemed to end, was larger than they had expected.

Upon filling their big camper-van with diesel they asked the man with oil on his hands where they might park overnight and where they might eat.

He looked at them oddly, suggested a place by the town creek for parking, that he thought was a public reserve but he wasn't sure. His suggestions for a meal ranged from a nice burger place where the 'mining crowd' go, to a sandwich shop or the supermarket that can provide a meal.

Finally, as he wiped his hands on a piece of rag, he added.

"If you want something a bit special. I mean really nice stuff then there's the 'Majestic'."

He paused.

"It's run by the tribe. They're fine cooks. A lot to do with our history I guess."

"History? What do you mean?"

"Oh, nothing. Influences. Stories. Just rumours. Silly stuff." There was the impression the mechanic had spoken out of turn. He had been lost in the moment and gone beyond a boundary.

"Who are the 'tribe?'"

He walked away with their payment in hand.

"The people who run this town," he remarked, over his shoulder. The visitors didn't see him smile.

The creek was surrounded by grass and willow trees.

"Bit of an oasis," said the man. "Wouldn't have expected this, out here. All empty rolling grassland on the way in and it's pretty much dry plains and dust past here I believe."

His wife set up the folding table outside their van while he unfolded two chairs. They drank tea and ate digestive biscuits as the sun lowered itself in the sky.

"Let's walk," the man said, "that hamburger cafe is up the street. We passed it when we came down here."

"Don't get many visitors here," the man behind the counter said. "This place is a dead end. Nowhere to go from here."

He was deftly constructing their hamburgers along with other orders. The chips bubbled in the fryer. The meat patties looked particularly thick and appeared to contain herbs and spices. The buns were a type of brioche.

"Oh, we like poking about. Try to stay away from the obvious and explore the unknown. Been retired for three years. My wife and I have found all sorts of interesting places and discovered many unusual histories by looking around in little odd places."

The man flipped over the meat patties and sliced steaks, cracked two eggs with his spare hand and gave a laugh. He shook his head.

"Well, this place might be a jackpot for you. Not that you'll ever know."

"A jackpot. Why is that? Is there some dark town legend waiting for me?"

The man slid a finished steak sandwich onto a plate, adding some chips, a sprinkle of salt then some salad and dressing.

He wiped a spot of oil from the edge of the plate and called the customer by name.

"What is it they say. Nothing to see here. Move along. Just

another town."

The man seated at the counter with his prim wife beside him, looked about at the various men and a few women, quietly eating and talking about the premises.

"Not what I expected. Aren't miners supposed to be boisterous and rowdy?"

The man placed two handsome hamburgers in front of the couple. Each had a toothpick through the centre holding the contents together.

"Not when you've got to be up early tomorrow to work. Anyway, our folk are different."

He moved away to take an order.

The two visitors ate their meal quietly. The hamburgers were unusually refined. A level of cuisine mostly reserved for an over-priced city establishment. They ordered some coffee while the proprietor busied himself with more hamburger orders and a round of pancakes. Even the pancakes were wafer-thin and done with lemon, spices and butter, dusted with a touch of fine sugar.

When it came time to pay they thanked the man for an excellent meal and said they would recommend his establishment.

As the man was about to leave he turned and asked another question.

"Ville Perdu. An unusual name for a town. It's French, isn't it? Do you know where the name came from and what it means.?"

The man smiled and tilted his head.

"It is a mystery, isn't it. Let me know if you get any leads."

In the morning, by the creek, magpies sang their gentle burbling call. The man sat at their little table and drank tea.

His bowl of muesli was finished. He was dressed in shorts and leather sandals with a smart green polo shirt that looked fresh. As he gazed about in the contented manner of one who enjoys the outdoors if it is kept at a safe distance, his wife emerged from their van.

"I thought I'd let you sleep a while longer."

"Thank you, dear. The birds are lovely to hear when you wake. I must say I'm surprised we're the only campers here."

The man twisted in his chair to look at his wife.

"This isn't a camping ground, it's just a bit of spare land next to the creek. I doubt there's any need for a camping ground."

"Do you think?"

"I'm sure of it. Who is going to drive all day toward the desert to a dead end that offers no promise of fulfillment then have to turn round and drive all the way back again? People like to pass through places rather than be trapped.

Nobody comes here unless they have no choice."

"We did."

The man scratched his temple.

"Yes .... we did. We're a lot more curious than most. I like to think of us as latter-day adventurers."

The man's wife lifted an empty orange juice carton.

"Or less sensible."

Taking a lead from his wife's displeasure the man took a notepad from his shirt pocket.

"I'll make a list for the supermarket."

"Don't forget your cap. You'll be complaining of a burnt head."

The man involuntarily touched his skull. A sore point that his wife used against him.

Alice watched them casually as they filled a shopping basket. They were the only customers at this hour. The man seemed a little brusque with his wife, deciding what they would purchase and what brand. He had a thin moustache and small beard that announced his demeanour before he spoke. Shorts, bony legs and leather sandals. Probably bald under his Panama hat. His wife was slightly dumpy in her yellow-flowered frock. She had no doubt grown used to his ways over their years together. Alice liked to study people. She was rarely wrong.

A man, perhaps in his late fifties, came in the door of the market and Alice reached behind her counter to a drip filter coffee machine. She poured the hot brew into a mug, added some cream and handed it to the man. He tipped his head in acknowledgment and smiled.

He walked slowly over to one of her window tables, seated himself easily and quietly sipped his brew, staring at the scene outside or waist in deep reflection. It was hard to tell.

The couple seemed to have completed their shopping. "Surprisingly well-stocked market," said the man appearing in front of the counter. "Interesting European items, pates, cheeses and such."

"You even have our favourite talcum powder," said the lady.

Alice nodded.

"We have the mining flights to thank for that. The planes always have a lot of spare room on their way back so the deliveries are pretty easy."

"So we could have flown here?"

"There's an occasional commercial flight that's once a week if there are enough passengers, which is not always the case. The miner's planes are strictly for the mines."

As Alice tallied up the purchases and packed them into

carry bags she waited for the first question. This man was a talker and he would want to ask questions. They were rare these visitors and mostly disappeared again within a day. She had a feeling this one was different.

He hitched his shorts up and gazed into the distance. Here it came.

"The mines are quite close to the town I noticed. There's no huge trucks or a rail line. How do they get the minerals out of here?"

"On the planes," Alice answered. She enjoyed holding back, waiting for the next question.

He hitched his shorts again then rubbed his chin.

"And umm so, what is it they mine?"

"Gold. Long thin reefs of gold. And blue/green sapphires." The man puffed up. He looked startled.

"I say, that's quite impressive. I've never heard of this. You'd assume it would be common knowledge. Why aren't the big mining giants in here?"

Alice placed the last itemof almond/apricot muesli in the man's carry bag and gave a knowing smile.

"Because a long time ago some very wise men noticed the potential of the area and stitched up the whole parcel in some very tight claims and leases. They are aboriginal sites. Not to be touched."

She paused, then handed over the last of the shopping bags.

"There is one big miner. They're in the process of going broke. They found a loophole in the legal structure and grabbed some land near the native mine. Found nothing."

The man's wife was anxious to leave but the man was too intense in his quest for answers.

"I worked for the Government," he said, with some gravitas. "On the legal side of things."

He paused for effect.

"I have not seen any aboriginal people hereabouts. Could this claim of theirs be a little dubious, shall we say?"

Alice leaned across the counter in a conspiratorial way.

"Over half the population here are aboriginal, sir. That gentleman over there enjoying his morning coffee is one of our senior and important first nation townsfolk."

The man and his wife both peered at the coffee drinker who now seemed absorbed in the book he was reading. Although for anybody who knew Grober they would have known he was hearing every word of the conversation at the counter and smiling quietly to himself.

"He doesn't seem very 'native', the man whispered back to Alice. He pursed his lips as if the whole concept was somehow distasteful.

"Whatever do you mean?" replied Alice, enjoying the exchange.

"Well ..... he's like us. He has the colouring of a chap who

may have just returned from a nice seaside holiday."
Alice drew back.
"Well, it's not for me to say, sir. Perhaps the local families
are not as coloured as some of their cousins from other
parts but I'm sure it's just the way things are. I suspect
they would be quite offended if you questioned their
heritage."
"Well," said the man, picking up his bags of groceries,
"Naturally we wouldn't want that but it is peculiar. It
intrigues me I must say."

Alice watched the couple walking away down the street,
deep in conversation.
"He's a little too curious for my liking," she said out loud.
The man Grober turned and looked at her.
"Yeah, we'll keep watching him."

By early afternoon the man and his wife had ascertained
that this town offered very little in entertainment,
landmarks, background or cultural events. Neat and well
presented, it was as if the place were a crime scene and all
the surroundings were not to be touched.
At least that was the impression the man offered his wife
as they ate their sandwiches on a quiet seat in the town's
small park.
They watched a mother with two preschool children

who happily swung backwards and forwards in the shiny
new playground area. The swings and the rest of the
playground were painted either red or yellow or black.
"Native flag colours," the man whispered. "Now are they
aboriginal? I can't tell."
"A very pretty family," his wife added.
"That one's a boy. You can't call boys pretty."
"Oh, you know what I mean. What's wrong with the
colours, do you say?"
"They're the same colours as used on the aboriginal flag.
I don't think that's a coincidence."
The wife flicked some crumbs down to a small bird
waiting expectantly at their feet.
"Well, the playground looks new and very nice. If these
hard to find aboriginals wanted those colours I can't
see the harm in that. Besides, the slide and the climbing
apparatus at the back are red, white and blue, so your
theory might be more of a coincidence."
The lady liked to have her little victories.
The man stood and brushed his shirt and shorts.
He glanced again at the people in the playground.
"It's all a bit odd. That's all I'm saying. Intriguing. I'd like
to know more. No harm in that. I shall set up my computer
this evening and connect to the world. See what's on
record."

They decided to try the Majestic Cafe for their evening
meal. The man felt the establishment might give him an
insight into the more moneyed members of the town's
population.

With its spacious dining area, rich dark timber bar and
trimmings and deep red wallpaper the interior came as a
surprise.

"Bit more than a cafe," the man opined as they waited at
the door. "Like a Parisian Gentlemen's Club. Quite an old
building it appears."

A young man named Phillipe, smartly dressed in black
trousers, a gleaming white shirt and a long dark green
apron, appeared and escorted them to a table by the
window. He presented them each with a menu, mentioned
the two specials and advised that he would be back
presently to take their order. Their drinks waiter would
speak to them soon.

"What a charming young man," said the wife. "Oh, I see
they have some type of salmon cakes. I might try them."
The man was glancing about, looking at the other guests,
the bar staff and trying to see into the kitchen.

"Was he one?"

"One what, dear?"

"You know. A native, a local. An aboriginal?"

"Who, Phillipe? I don't know dear. Let's see, he had dark
curly hair, a healthy complexion and a lovely smile.

He wore a wedding ring. So it's possible. What are you going to eat?"

The man ran his finger down the laminated pages.

"Beef and burgundy pie sounds pretty good."

Another waiter appeared at their table.

"Sorry for the holdup folks. Quite busy tonight. My name is Joshua. Now, what drinks can I get for you."

Joshua's knowledge of wine was impressive. They settled on a mid-priced bottle of Cabernet-merlot.

When Joshua returned and poured their wine. the man, sipped the offering and gave his approval, then asked his question.

"Are you aboriginal?"

Joshua paused, then smiled. He could have been Phillipe's brother except that his hair was quite light and in a ponytail.

"Yes, I suppose I am sir."

Staring back into the young man's eyes the customer squirmed in his seat.

"I meant no offence. Are you local? It's just that I've noticed you chaps don't seem very aboriginal. In the traditional sense. If you know what I mean?"

He waved his arms about in an effort to appear nonplussed.

It was an opportunity to make the man squirm even more but Joshua refrained.

"We have dwelt here in this land for many thousands of years I believe. So yes, we are local. If that is all, sir?"

Joshua's manner was so impeccably pleasant.

With the young man now attending to a table on the other side of the room, the man leaned across to his wife.

"Was he rude by being overly polite.?"

"You are rather abrupt."

The man sat back a little.

"Be that as it may I can't wait to return to our van and get online. There are things to be looked into. This is fascinating. I need to find out more. There is a strange reluctance to discuss matters. Also, there are odd bits of French culture here and there. And I'm rather sure I'm hearing little hints of French accents. Even with the so-called natives. Why, I ask? Do you know the town's name Ville Perdu means 'Lost Town'?

His wife nodded and smiled wanly.

"Rather appropriate I suppose. Let's enjoy our meal first, shall we."

She looked about casually and added.

"Anyway, I'm sure a I heard a chap with an Irish accent on our walk up here. This is a multicultural country after all."

After a cup of tea, the woman patted her husband's shoulder and said goodnight.

Squeezed into the van's small alcove seat and table he

nodded back but his face returned to the screen of his laptop computer. With his satellite dish on the roof of the van, he was connected to the world. He did not come to bed until past one a.m.

In the morning he was up early. He ate his muesli outside at their little table, surrounded by a pleasant chorus of birds greeting the day. His focus was on his satellite phone beside his coffee cup. At two minutes past nine a.m., he made his first call. He had contacts. People who knew situations and how to circumnavigate obstacles. Record keepers and government middlemen who had access to information.

By late morning his fat notebook and folder had many pages of notations.

The town had suddenly come into existence in the latter part of the 1800s. A rather rapid rise from nothing to a functioning town. It did not slowly attract a large population, it seemed to just happen. There were only a few photos of the period. Taken to support a Native Claim on the area. At the time, such claims were deemed frivolous and almost unworthy of serious consideration but due to its remoteness and apparent lack of any known value of the land, the claim was given some legal credence. It was noted by those who later examined the documentation that the 'natives' had presented a surprisingly astute case for their claim with quite strong but subtle clauses that guaranteed the sanctuary. It was to use the parlance 'ironclad'.

Initially, it was suspected they had received help from some parties with vested interests but none could be found.

Years later, when native title laws came into existence the whole area was locked up tightly, in what was once again described as a masterful presentation with every position and eventuality covered in detail.

The man found the archived title. He was impressed by its completeness.

It made him more curious. What powers were at play in this strange end-of-the-road hamlet? He wanted to know more, much more. His quest became obsessive.

At well after one p.m. the two people made their way into the town and up to the little supermarket on the street that sloped up the hill.

Alice was ringing up an array of items for a customer with two more behind, each with a loaded trolley.

"Hmm, bad timing," the man muttered. He fronted up to Alice and caught her attention.

"Do you do lunch?"

"If you're willing to wait. Sandwiches, pies, simple grills, that sort of thing. The menus are on the tables."

Over half an hour later Alice carried a tray to a table by the shop's windows.

"Sorry for the delay. All here now."

"That's quite okay my dear. Nice to watch the passing parade," offered the woman. "Do you work here alone?"

Alice stopped.

"No, I have three girls who do unpacking, shelves, cooking and other chores."

"Native girls?"

Alice looked a little annoyed.

"Two are first nation. And then one is European. They take turns to be in charge when we're away. Okay, yours was the toasted cheese and tomato sandwich and yours, sir, was the chicken pie. Here's your pot of tea and the milk. Enjoy."

"Looks delicious," the man said.

Before Alice could retreat he added, "This town fascinates me."

"Really."

"How can it support several mines and not attract any interest from elsewhere?"

Alice sighed.

"I explained that previously sir, The mining rights are all owned by the local people. What exactly is your interest? Do you have a background in mining?"

The man took a mouthful of his pie.

"Oh damn, that is good. Can't beat homemade. If you made this I congratulate you. For a country town, the food here is exceptional. I mean oddly good. Why is it so good? Some tradition? What? No, I'm not in mining. I'm a retired lawyer. I did corporate work. I still dabble. So, as I said, I just find situations ..... well, fascinating. I've just got to know more. Can't help myself. It's the way I am."

Later that afternoon the man called Grober rang a number on his phone.

"Hi Moorant, can we meet. It will be necessary. We'll need four to do this properly."

At sunset, the tourist took all his paperwork, his laptop computer and his phone and stacked them on the table in his van.

Then he and his wife walked away in the direction of the Majestic Cafe. So impressed with their previous night's meal they were looking forward to indulging once again.

They were given a table in a corner beside the rich crimson window drapes.

"Feel these." His wife stroked the material. "Such quality. Very odd."

"Indeed," said the man.

The meal was superb. Both chose more adventurous

items and were delighted that the food was not at all strange. They were filled with goodwill and decided to leave a tip which was not their normal practice.

Both Phillipe and Joshua had been particularly attentive all evening. Joshua even presented them each with a small digestif drink at the conclusion of their meal and Phillipe had followed up with complimentary coffee.

"When visitors start to become regulars we like to look after them," he explained

"What lovely people," said the man's wife as they strolled back to their van by the creek. The streets were mostly empty. The town was at peace.

At one point the man stumbled.

"I think I may have taken in a little too much red wine," he said, with a laugh.

Once inside they sat for a moment. The man with his head bowed. He then looked up, blinking in the light.

"I'm looking forward to tomorrow. This town has so many oddities that need to be explored. It's not right you know. I will be asking a lot of questions I tell you."

He paused.

"Do you know that late last night and all today's walking has made me quite tired. I can hardly stay awake."

His wife looked at him blankly.

"You're right. We must be unfit. I am quite befuddled.

Can't think which way is up."

By 9p.m. they were both deeply asleep.

In the large highway town of Ravensburg, the caravan
park is extensive, running to large lawned areas and
occasional trees. For those wishing to find an isolated
spot, it is quite easy to be away from any noisy, happy
campers and have your own peaceful patch.

This morning was bright and fresh. A seamless blue sky
was already emerging from the pink dawn when the door
of a large campervan, parked under a fine river gum,
opened and a man stood in the frame and looked around.
He squeezed his eyes a number of times in an attempt to
focus then gazed about for some time. He scratched his
nose. After a moment he rubbed his face vigorously as if
trying to summon up a greater level of consciousness.
He cautiously walked down the van's step and with hands-
on-hips. He examined his van. He walked around his
vehicle. He looked up at the tree then away to the distant
office building shading his eyes, taking his time.

On his little table next to the van was a crumpled copy of
the weekly Ravensburg Herald. It was dated two days ago.
The man peered at the paper for some time then sat down
heavily on one of the seats, immediately realising it was
wet with overnight dew. The man was rather wild-eyed.
Now the man's wife came down the steps of the van onto

the soft grass, timidly stepping with bare feet. She too was in her night attire and looked puzzled.

"What day is it, dear?"

The man stared at her open-mouthed for ten seconds.

"I don't know," he said at last, "It might be Friday. I need a calendar."

"Well I am very worried," said the woman, "I have no recollection of us arriving here."

She gazed about as if viewing her surroundings for the first time.

"Isn't that odd? Nothing is familiar. Yet there's a booking slip on the table inside. If Friday is correct we've been here four days. We've got some shopping bags inside from Ravensburg Market. We must have been there. Is it possible I've had a stroke? Perhaps I should see a doctor. What do you think? Do you recall? You must know. Tell me what we've been doing?" Her voice was tremulous.

The man shook his head. He looked angry. His head shaking continued.

"Dammit. I've got exactly the same problem. We couldn't both have conveniently had a stroke at the same time."

He hunched his shoulders and looked about the park, giving occasional grunts. His wife waited dutifully. After a minute he banged his fist on the table.

"I think we're the victims of somebody's practical joke. I'll bet there are some drug-taking louts in this camp who thought it would be funny to pop an hallucinogenic compound into our meal or something. I'm going to have some breakfast and go looking for them. That's what I'm going to do, I tell you."

The man's wife sat down in their other chair then winced as the cold moisture soaked into her nightie.

"That may not be possible. There's a printout of our booking for tonight at Berrington Motel up the highway. We'll have to get going before lunch if we're going enjoy the drive".

The man looked exasperated.

"A motel? Berrington? Well, it is the next stop. Nowhere else to go. I do remember driving into this place. But when? I've been in a place for four days and I have no idea if I enjoyed myself, I do worry. Is it medical? Something we ate? A drug or trick? Is somebody here, right now, watching us and laughing? I don't know. Let's throw out all our food and buy some more. We'll make a pact to watch each other to see if this happens again."

The man continued to make sweeping head movements as though he might yet catch the perpetrators of their dilemma.

To his left, to his right, the place presented calm, well mown grassy expanses of empty early morning silence.

That night, sitting at the table in his motel suite, fresh

from a shower in a real bathroom and able to remember every event in his day, the man opened his laptop computer.

After looking around on the screen he called to his wife. "Seems we were out and about in Ravensburg. There's a file full of photos I've taken. Looks like a nice place. This memory thing is ridiculous. Should I be worried, angry, scared or unconcerned?"

"Any nice pictures of me?"

"No, seems I only took landmarks and scenery."

THE WHITE BOY

Big and self-important. He approached with a manner of
one who has a distasteful errand that must be carried out.
"You, head wants to see you."
He stood with his hands on his hips.
"Now."
"Ooohh," said a couple of my year, sitting on a bench
across the little courtyard.
Some of the older boys engaged in their responsibilities
with humility and respect for those about them. This one
did not.
I stood and brushed some lunchtime sandwich crumbs
from my uniform. Waited a moment then lifted my head

and looked at him. Smiled slowly. Spoke directly.

"I know the way. Thank you for your assistance."

He flushed. Probably wanted to hit me but such an action would have 'consequences'.

"Well, get a move on," he called to my back.

As I made my way across the quadrangle, squared off on all sides by impressive stone buildings and much history I pondered the reason for the call-up. On a scholarship and only six months into the first year, I had been before the head twice. My father was horrified. Relieved of caring for his son after my mother's cancer, the thought of me being returned as unsuitable or lacking some intangible quality left him constantly on edge.

Both occasions had concerned quite minor deviations from the protocol. One for writing a slightly scathing essay concerning race relations instead of 'sticking to historical facts' and the second for bucking the college system by telling a senior that he could not order me around. It turned out that college etiquette did give him such privileges.

It occurred to me then that my position as a 'charity case' might be better served if I lost some of my 'attitude'. Being intelligent was not a major advantage in such a place. Actually, it could almost be seen as a hindrance. Lately, I had applied more effort to flying below the radar, considering that not being noticed was a good thing. Once applied I found it was possible to be near invisible to the older boys who were generally motivated by knocking down any sign of confidence shown by the younger set.

My gentle knock and polite entry to the head's large office produced not a look of foreboding but a rather regal beckoning wave of the hand and welcoming smile.
He seemed pleased to see me, bade me forward across the carpet and oriental rug to take a seat on the opposing side of his substantial carved desk. He had all the paraphernalia of the main man in a prestigious school.
An ornate inkstand complete with a full ink receptacle, a large leather-edged writing pad, even an oriental jade figurine. The latter no doubt of some importance in his family history. I looked in vain for the pen that he might employ in his inkstand but it was not at large on his desktop.
"Ah, lad, make yourself comfortable. We have a matter to discuss. Fear not, it is of a pleasing nature. Our mental capacities must be applied to an upcoming event and you may be the very person who can assist me in providing the most acceptable and might I say beneficial answer."
His words seemed rehearsed. They made little sense except that I perhaps was about to be set up in some scheme that would extract him from a dilemma.

Despite my suspicion, I couldn't help but like the man with his flowery speech patterns and 'can do' approach to life.

Even my previous two meetings with him had been based on positivity rather than reprimands. Short of being caught in the act of murder or such, I'd known I was not in any real danger. Scholarship boys must be seen to succeed. It was good for the school's reputation. Paying students would not have been spoken to at all. But I needed to be guided. My father understood none of this. He was a good man, an academic man, just not a man that had any great interest in children. I was a burden to his ongoing ambitions and my being elsewhere suited him immensely.

The discussion with the headmaster this morning involved a new student shortly to become a member of the revered college ranks. His name was 'Stephen'. He was from a central desert tribe. Despite the obvious disadvantages of his geographical position I was told, he had excelled at school, achieved remarkable scores in all his exam results and thus had been awarded the college's first 'special' scholarship aimed at encouraging talented 'first nation' students. Other institutions were involved in the scheme from some years back and the results were generally very rewarding. No doubt assured that the whole process would reflect favourably on the college, we had now joined in with a minimum number of one. Hardly an indication of our goodwill and largesse but there was a great deal of college reputation to be considered in any move they made.

From this first venture into the plan, it seemed that its success or otherwise would to a great degree rest on my shoulders.

The head did not specifically place the burden on my shoulders but I felt it arrive as he spoke.

His reasons for 'honouring' me with a full-time caretaking role were to do with the contents of my misguided essay which indicated my 'strong feelings regarding race relations' and my obvious strength of character and decision-making skills. The compliments flowed. I was definitely being set up.

He then added the clincher.

"As a scholarship student yourself you would be best placed to appreciate its special purpose and thus guide 'Stephen' and be his mentor and companion .... "

Guide, mentor? The head's opinion or hopes exceeded my expectations by a considerable margin.

At this point, I quietly offered up a small prayer that this Stephen person and I would find each other agreeable company. If not, my time here could be miserable.

Of course, the head failed to mention in his lengthy sales

pitch that I had a quite advanced ability to read between the lines.

None of the fee-paying college students would even consider such a proposal. Their wealthy parents would be suitably annoyed/offended. The college for them was a place to establish one's position. To stake a claim on the social ladder and most of all to make contacts. Those that would be needed in a future life in business and commerce.

With a powerful old stone and ivy establishment such as this, one's place was booked at birth and the wearing of the black blazer with its distinctive yellow piping and pocket crest and the school tie was very much a door to a known and planned pathway.

As a scholarship student, I owed the college some loyalty. (My whole kit including two uniform sets had been provided, presumably to save any chance that I may look a little frayed at the edges and not fit in.)

Gratitude required payment in kind. This was my penance. A form of payback for their grace.

None of this was spoken. I knew and the head knew that I knew.

He thanked me for taking on the task, though I don't recall any options being offered and extended his hand for a warm handshake. The deal was sealed.

It was midweek when Stephen arrived and the first
surprise occurred. I had expected a quite dark-skinned
chap with a desert-dust squint in his eyes.

Stephen was quite handsome. The college uniform gave
him an exotic persona. He seemed more like a male model
with a good tan.

I felt a pang of guilt for my racial expectations although I
wondered if a darker complexion would have suited the
program's aims with greater clarity and purpose. Many
of the ultra-rich Asian students were more obvious than
Stephen.

He was polite to a fault and compliant with my wishes
regarding our shared room. I introduced him to a few of
the less entitled members of our year. He seemed at ease
with them. While not displaying an air of superiority he
gave off an unfussed charm that left them generally silent.
In fact, they appeared intimidated.

We spent time together in classes, lectures and the dining
hall. Discussion subjects seemed easy to find despite the
gap in our backgrounds.

Over the next few days, I discovered two other things
about Stephen that made him a grand companion.

I found he had that special connection with the land that
we white folk do not possess. A gift we should at least
admire and try to understand.

Secondly, he had a wonderful sense of humour. Not brash loud guffaw humour but a quiet observational wit that I so enjoyed. He noticed things that I entirely missed.

Put simply Stephen and I were a match. Except that he was academically superior, we were a great team of two with so many compatible characteristics. My assignment to be his friend, companion and minder was proving easy because I liked the guy.

I had to assume he liked me. He was enigmatic after all. Finally, I decided that no person, no matter how confident and at ease with their fellow humans could keep up a pretence of bonhomie over an extended period without some cracks appearing.

We became known as the odd couple. Wondering if I should be offended by the title I found it had nothing to do with ethnicity and was based on me being fiercely blonde and cream coloured while Stephen had more of an average complexion. A normal kid. I was the 'odd' of the mix.

The head hovered discreetly. No doubt the board of curmudgeons and relics were keen to have this radical departure from school norms turn into a triumph for their flirtation with progressive thinking.

He ambushed me on the way to the pool change rooms. A contrived accidental encounter,

"Ah lad, how fortunate, been meaning to say hello. Well, now, the question on everybody's lips, how is Stephen settling in? Is he content? Good room companion? Any concerns that may need addressing?"

"Not a one, sir. Excellent, tidy, thoughtful roommate. Stephen is a happy chap as far as I can tell."

"As far as you can tell?"

"I mean there are no issues. He likes it here."

The head looked at me as if I might be leading him on, telling him what he wanted to hear rather than the cold hard truth. He seemed to decide that I was a purveyor of truth.

"You two enjoying each other's company then?"

"Yes Sir, quite a lot."

"Well, that's splendid. I do see you out and about together quite often. Getting along. Pals, mates. You mustn't keep him all to yourself you know. It is important that he mingles. Meets lots of his school chums."

"I'll address the mingling issue forthwith, sir."

"Grand," said the head. patting my shoulder. "Off to swimming I see. Keep an eye on Stephen. I'm not sure of his swimming abilities, being from the desert and all."

"He swims quite well, sir."

The head looked a little surprised.

"Well, there you are. Splendid."

He wandered off, his hands clasped behind his back.

Perhaps deep in thought, perhaps not.

Mingling was not high on my agenda. It would serve little purpose in such an institution. Besides, Stephen did not give the impression he was here to 'connect' and conquer the world of commerce. Just the learning aspects of the college. He seemed to operate on a higher plane. One that I was yet to come to terms with.

Thirteen-year-olds in their first year are at the bottom rung of a carefully constructed ladder in private colleges. The system does not allow for a deviation of any degree. However, being paired with the strange, supposedly coloured, scholarship person meant we both were largely ignored. In a way, it was a peaceful life. We were spared the system of ritualistic behaviour designed to put students in their place and mark them by some vague value of their worth. Possibly the head had put out a word that the college's first native scholarship recipient must be a success or it was just the 'system' working away as it had done to numerous others beforehand.
By what means our isolation was achieved I was quite content with the netherworld in which Stephen and I existed.
Did he notice?

Relaxed, laying on our backs beside the lake, during a free period, I skirted the subject. I gazed out across the glassy water, the impressive array of grand old stone college buildings in the distance.

"A different world to your country." By which I meant his tribal country.

"Not so different as you might imagine my friend."

Not the answer I expected but Stephen was mysterious, to say the least. Perhaps a more direct approach.

"You swim really well. Where did you learn?"

"In one of our swimming places."

I had him. I thought he was unaware of my prep work before his arrival. When assigned to be Stephen's bodyguard I'd done some rough research. He came from a remote town that appeared to be on the edge of grassy hinterland before the start of a more arid desert-like country. The limited information I found concentrated on the open plains while failing to mention that the town itself had a substantial creek. Even so, our exchange that day gave rise to the possibility of something more.

"I believe there is no water bigger than a puddle where you come from."

"Yes, there is. "

"And where might that be?"

"I can't tell you."

"Why?"

"It's a secret."

"You've got some hidden billabong?"

"Oh, you can't begin to understand."

"I thought I was your friend."

"You are, white boy. One of the nicest, most decent people I have ever met but I can't go against our law."

"Ah, tribal stuff."

"If you like. Something along those lines."

"What? An even deeper secret?"

I was about to be flippant then I glanced at his face. He seemed torn, even sad. The subject was serious.

"I respect your wishes, Stephen. Can I ask again at some future date?"

He looked me over as if trying to decide whether any further correspondence was possible, then nodded.

"Yes, you can."

The day was particularly hot. We had walked around the far side of the lake on the school grounds. The sides of the lake were edged by a series of willow trees. They reached down to the grass and provided a wall to hide us from the far side. No other students seemed to bother with stepping out or going anywhere much away from the comforts of the college buildings. We had the area to ourselves.

School rules required full uniform at all times when

outside the classrooms. For the non-boarders that included travel to and from the school grounds.

"Damn that water looks nice," I said.

"Yeah, it really does," Stephen replied.

We looked at each other.

"Let's do it."

We stripped to our underwear.

I caught Stephen looking at me.

"What?"

"Nothing really. Just each time I see you ….. You know friend you have incredibly pale skin. I mean fit and healthy and all that, just …. well really light. No spots, freckles, marks. Why is that? Are you made of marble or something? You get in the sun enough. Is it in your ancestry?

Stephen stopped.

"I'm sorry. That's rather rude isn't it".

I looked at my stomach and arms.

"No offence Stephen. I know I'm a bit see-through. Apparently, I have French ancestry. Don't know the details but I guess I'm not meant to be here in a country where the sun shines.

When I go to the doctor he says he can examine my internal organs because he can see them."

"You're making that bit up," said Stephen.

"Yes, I am."

We slid quietly into the water. Keeping close to the overhanging willow fronds we dived and explored the reeds and mysteries of the lake bottom. It was clear and surprisingly unpolluted. No debris, just a little plant life and the occasional fish. While surfacing and spitting out a mouthful of the lake water, it occurred to me that I was unaware of the origins of the lake's water supply. We were after all in a semi-urban environment. Would we succumb to a mysterious stomach malady?

The swim was quick so as not to be late for our next class. Drying off as best we could I considered that swimming in the lake may be forbidden. The college had two Olympic size pools after all. I had never seen anybody do so, only the rowing sculls seemed to use it. I commented to Stephen that no doubt some senior will have seen us and be considering reporting our behaviour.

"I don't know," he said, "We seem immune."

"Oh, so you have noticed."

Stephen sat on the bank in the sun. He looked at the sky.

"Of course, I've noticed. I almost feel cheated that we've become untouchables."

"Maybe untouchable is a bit extreme. I'm sure we'd get sorted out if we crossed some ritualistic unseen line and upset the senior, entitled chaps."

Stephen put his hand up.

"Maybe not. I can see how this works. When I went for my interview for this place, there were two of us. Me, an aboriginal with all his colour washed out or a suitably pale brown something and this other fella from up north who was full-blood. He was a genius. He ticked every box. Very articulate. Nice guy. Charming and confident. Destined for great things. I'm pretty sure the committee recommended him for the scholarship. I then think the representative from this college vetoed the decision. I can only guess he thought I'd be less noticeable and blend in more. Be nice for the press release but not controversial. So yes, I've noticed. I know I'm an experiment. One that could be dropped at any time."

I looked at Stephen for a moment.

"Wow. I'm just some lucky white boy with a scholarship. You're a whole damned experiment."

Stephen was silent for a moment. Had I made an inappropriate joke?

Then he laughed. A lot.

The term results came out. The head cornered me while on a quiet walk to meet Stephen at the cafeteria. He had a talent for appearing from nowhere and making the crossing of paths seem totally casual.

"Ah, lad."

My name seemed to have escaped him once more.

"I was very pleased to see your improved results in the latest figures. You're matching it with your good friend Stephen. Ahem, near the top of your year. Now let me see...... is he dragging you up or are you dragging him down? Must be the former, eh?"

He rubbed his chin, then stated the obvious.

"I'm joking, of course, my boy. We're all delighted with how the ... the ..... "

"Experiment?"

He looked shocked, slightly annoyed.

"No, no. The benefits, yes, the benefits are shaping up."

I stayed silent.

He gave me a friendly half nod.

"Well, carry on."

Another pat on the shoulder. I sometimes thought he'd like to give me a fatherly hug.

I told Stephen.

"Yes, the head grabbed me too, in the library. Had a whispered chat. He's very happy that we're doing well. Wanted to know if I still got along with you. I said 'no'. I couldn't stand you anymore."

"I'm sure you did."

"One of the rugby team guys smirked after he'd left. He said, 'Friends in high places, you'll go far.'

I looked at Stephen.

"It's students like him that means we'll never be top of our year. Almost certainly they fudge the figures. Probably not ours but the wealthy and the connected would need to see that their son was doing well. Not sure what they do about the seriously cognitively challenged but no doubt there's a formula."

Suddenly the term was ending and the summer break loomed. Stephen caught me looking at the calendar above my desk. I could feel his eyes wandering over me as I tried to concentrate.
"Why are you staring at me? You do that a lot you know."
He continued to look, frozen, on the side of his bed. I noted that his mind was elsewhere. Then he snapped back.
"Sorry, indecision. Wrestling with a problem."
"Can I help?"
"You are the problem, white boy."

The scholarship's from our college included a reasonable allowance for travel in our holiday period.
We had taken a coach as far inland as could be arranged then picked up a little cloud-bouncing charter to the town. Stephen's town. It lay beneath us now as we circled to line up our final approach.
"Bigger than I thought, this place of yours."

Stephen looked at me.

"Yeah, it's huge."

He paused, looking at me as he had done many times over the last few days. I was a giant puzzle apparently but he wouldn't say why.

"Listen, this is something I just have to know. I can't work out the feeling but it's there. Please tell me again. Tell me you'll understand if they say no."

"Stephen, you've told me about ten times. You have this intuition happening and like an itch that needs to be scratched, here we are. I am the itch. If it comes to nothing, I'll be on the next plane out of town. I'll see you back at school, to resume our studies.
We'll still be friends and life will go on."

Why I was here instead of at home in the city suburbs with my father and sister was all due to a whimsical moment from Stephen. Without authorisation, he had crossed some boundary and invited me to come with him to his town and to a place he could not tell me about but he so much wanted me to see.

He had made the decision based on my surname, a theory he mapped out and the fact that he believed in some force of nature that was influencing our paths.

Its beginnings were rooted in his interest in my past.

It gathered momentum the day I revealed my name was

actually Marcel Proulx and that it had switched to the surname of my adoptive parents after they had taken me in at the age of four.

My real parents were unknown to me. My sister was also adopted. When my adoptive mother died my adoptive father found solace in never being home. He busied himself with his work and numerous activities that kept him away. He was a nice man, a kind man but displays of affection just alluded him. My scholarship at a boarding school was a blessing. He was so happy. My welfare was provided for without the necessity of too much family interaction. Thus being absent during school holidays would cause no concern at all.

Now Stephen's great mystery awaited. He wanted to ask somebody about my name. It seemed to hold great importance. Historical significance he would not explain. If I had been asked to describe Stephen at this stage I would have said my name scared him a little. Whether I would be welcome or shunned and rejected, depended on Stephen and his ability to sell me as a trustworthy, sympathetic soul who would die rather than reveal the secret. White people he said were kept at bay. Not included or trusted in this town, even though relations were harmonious. But exceptions were sometimes made.

Throughout the early part of the Stephen narrative, I had the impression that all he told me was not true. The story seemed to be moulded and adjusted to suit the circumstances. Who ran the town, how it functioned, what sort of town it was and where did these mysteries all fit in were all subjects left unexplained.

There was a slight bump and the pilot rolled us and our four other passengers up to a single hangar that served as the town's airport infrastructure.
"Nice landing."
Stephen moved out onto the little set of stairs beside the plane. He looked over his shoulder.
"He does this run a lot. A helluva lot."
Now I felt uneasy. Though I noted the pilot was a white guy and possibly half the other passengers. Were we all not welcome?

At 11am I was left alone in a small store. A sort of market with shelves of cans and jars and shopping trolleys. It had three sets of tables and chairs near the front windows. A very bright place to view the street and the inhabitants in their environment. Stephen had decided he would rather park me in this place than to take me home, just yet.
In the shop, a lady, whose name was Alice, had talked me

into a cold bottle of ginger beer.

"Best drink for thirst on a warm day," she said. "Mind you, it's pretty much the only kind of day we have."

"This is Marcel," Stephen had mentioned to Alice as he headed off out the door.

Seated, staring out the window at a largely empty street, I could tell she was watching me as she served a customer. When they'd gone she walked over and sat down. She leaned on the table her chin resting on her hands as she looked me over. It was a little off-putting. I thought of Stephen doing the same thing. Was I that fascinating?

"Drink okay?"

"Um yes. Very nice, thank you."

"You came in with Stephen."

"Um, yes."

"Don't say Um sweetie. You're a college boy. Do you know him?"

"Stephen, yes. We're roommates at college. And friends."

"Ahh," she said. "We're all very proud of Stephen. Smart boy. So, you're here with Stephen."

"Yes, I'm here with Stephen."

"Your name is Marcel."

"Yes, it is."

She stopped and looked at me as if examining a specimen. This ongoing obsession of late.

"Blonde curly hair," she muttered. "I wonder. He may be

onto something. He's bright and it does seem to be on ongoing occurrence."

"Pardon?"

Alice snapped out of here reverie.

"Oh nothing dear. Just ah ……. ruminating."

She stared at me again.

"You do know he's going to be away from here soon, for most of the holiday break? You may be left alone a fair bit."

It was an uneasy moment. I could only look back at her. Our eyes were locked. Sweat trickled down my neck. I sipped my ginger beer. Moments dripped past. Her stare was like a tiny inquisition. Then she slowly turned her head with an odd quizzical look. Her hand went to her mouth. She looked back at me.

"How much of a friend is Stephen?"

I looked straight back at her.

"Since you ask. It's like I've found my lost brother. He thinks we're connected. Fateful or something. I'm really not sure what he's on about. He tells me vague stories that make no sense."

"Oh hell," she said, "What's your name?"

"Marcel. I told you."

"Marcel what?"

"Marcel Carpenter. Originally it was Proulx."

The lady continued to stare. She gave a slight half-laugh.

"Proulx eh. The little sailor boy."

"What?"

"Nothing. Just musing."

"Why do people want to know my name?"

Now Alice sat back. She looked up and about the ceiling.

"Oh my God," she said slowly, "He's going to ask isn't he."

It was a statement rather than a question.

After quite a time of silence where she stared out the window in an out-of-focus way, she stood to greet a new customer. Leaning down to me across the table she brushed her hand over my cheek and through my hair. She whispered, "Oh you're a peach Marcel. Sit here and pray you get Auntie Grace because Grober won't like you."

"Why won't he like me?" I whispered back.

"Because you're too damned white, Sweetness," she whispered breathily in my ear. "Even for one of the Frenchies."

Twenty minutes later Stephen came into the shop.

He nodded to Alice as he walked to my table.

Leaning over up close he said, "Come with me, It's critical. Auntie Grace wants to meet you."

As I made my way out behind Stephen I looked at Alice over at her checkout counter.

"Auntie Grace," I mouthed silently to her.

She gave me one of those fifty-percent chance looks.

I can now tell you that I have been to the place and the magic now owns me. Anything more I cannot, no, I will not say.

When I entered her small, neat house, Auntie Grace had looked up from her position on a big comfortable lounge and stared stoney-faced. Then she burst out laughing. It was a weazing, deep rumble.

"She used to smoke a lot," said Stephen out the corner of his mouth.

Still, her laughter continued. She was highly amused by my presence. And my appearance. I was not sure whether I should be flattered or annoyed that my appearance caused such a reaction.

Grober tolerates me. Makes numerous remarks about the magnanimous gesture by the 'first nation' people. He calls me 'white boy' or 'token boy'.

Says, "Still don't know how you did it. We gonna get diluted even more."

All this banter is unfair because I now know it is a partnership and both sides contribute equally.

At other times he calls me 'midshipman'. When I said I've never been near any boats, he said mysteriously,

"Oh yes, you have young sonny boy. You just don't

remember yet."

What can that mean? There's much more to know.

Alice told me that he likes me. It's all bluster. I wouldn't have been allowed in if they didn't trust me. I'm part of the ongoing search. The 'collection'.

What is the 'collection'? The ones they are not certain about. Where there is a connection but some doubt. For me, it is their belief that none of this is chance. Stephen and I were meant to meet. That, and my name.

It is why Grober tells the others that I should be watched. "Don't let the blonde hair and the pretty looks distract you. Clever words can hide deeper plans."

He says these things in front of me. Questions my 'credentials'. Laughs a little but will not explain what he means. What 'plans' could I possibly have

My real family is part of their quest. Not my other family. My original name may be a coincidence they say. Then they hint that it is not. It cannot be because I am one of them. One of the originals.

"He was, pardon is, a handsome lad and blonde. There is no argument there."

What do they mean? Was or is?

It has to do with the past and my affinity with the sea.

Something they say will come again.

All this mysterious talk while

I am welcomed in and shown their world but kept aside.

I suspect they feel I cannot be trusted yet. They are
wrong.
The secret remains. Their secret. My secret.

THE VILLAGE

A half days walk from the town, on a short but sharp incline, the horse could move no more. It was a good and loyal animal, well-fed and cared for most completely but the load was such that it could not muster further strength to assist its master in his quest.

The master and his assistant sat on the bank of grass beside the road while the horse, after a brief period of silent guilt at being unable to carry out its task, now grazed on some white flowers that were within its reach. The two men had their heads in their hands, pondering their predicament. The light was already moving toward midday. On their long sturdy cart behind their horse lay

a giant length of oak, cut and shaped. Skillfully joined
with wooden pegs to form an arm of a giant curve.
It was the first of four such sections to complete an
arched construction, made to order for the man at the
performer's building.
They would be paid upon completion. Paid well if their
work was satisfactory. It could lead to further work in
time.
They hoped, somewhat optimistically, that another cart
or animal might pass by and be able to offer assistance.
Only this one hill. After the slope was conquered it was a
gentle, pleasant roll, all the way into the village and then
left, over the creek to the large open area that was the
special world of magic and wonder where the 'Interprètes'
lived and practiced their art and skills.

This road was rarely travelled. The carpentry experts had
purchased their land quite cheaply some years before.
A farmer would not want a forest. However, for two young
men with an eye on a future in woodworking skills, it gave
them ample land and a wonderful supply of timber. Only
two actual farmers lived along this road. A road they had
practically created themselves in their younger days. Now
they were older and travelled less. The road was not ideal.
Consideration was given to going back and borrowing
one of the farmer's old paddock horses in the hope that

it might assist their beast to the top of the hill. It was not
a good solution. The horses they had in mind were past
working, just waiting to die.

The two men were glum. Their first chance at establishing
their credentials with these circus people was fading.
They would be known as unreliable. Further work for
these fussy, exacting folk would pass them by once the
word came of their inability to deliver.

In a sea of gloom, they waited for an answer that their
hearts told them was not available. Each, quietly searched
their brains for a hidden solution or trick or plan that may
yet save the day. Ropes and pulleys would be a way to
assist but they had neither.

The day was hot. One of the men stood and hitched his
trousers. He grunted and walked to the cart.

"One of us could ride to town and confess our failure," he
suggested.

"Will they cancel the order or find sympathy? I don't their
character that well."

In the silence and receiving no reply, he lifted a large
earthenware jar, wrestled the cork loose and drank the
cool water within. Tipping the jar he splashed some water
on his hands and wiped his face. Cold water to cool his
mood.

He called to his companion to ask if he wanted a drink.

The friend turned and did not reply. Instead, he waved his hand in an up and down motion, indicating that they should be quiet.

The friend stood, his head cocked as if listening to the air about, then in a further gesture of inquiry placed his hand behind his ear.

He gave a grunt and climbed further up the grass bank. Once more he cupped his ears.

Then the man with the water jug heard it too. Somebody or something was approaching from the direction of the village.

They waited, one gazing from the grassy bank, the other, still holding the jug, stood facing the road up over the hill. A steady sound. Not hurried but purposeful. They stared at the flickering peak of the hill. What could it be? Who would be on this road?

His head appeared first. Odd and swimming in the heat haze. A dot of black hair. He appeared far too high as if he might be flying. The two men waiting, squinted at the scene trying to make sense of what approached. Then the apparition grew. His torso rose slowly into view over the hill. He was bare-chested soaking up the midday sun. His baggy breeches were tied with a bright red sash. His eyes were closed.

When he opened them, he raised one fist to the sky in

triumph.

"Et te voila," he shouted. "Salut Monsieur Gerard. Nous sommes venus pour vous sauver."

It was the boy from the circus folk. A boy who scared them a little. The special boy. He appeared to have the gift of fortune-telling and seeing the future. He knew things that no one could conjure up by trickery. A quiet boy normally. One they avoided.

"Come to save us?" thought Gerard. He shrugged his shoulders to Christo on the bank.

How could an eight-year-old save them?

They waited. Soon, like a strange pantomime, it all became clear. As the calves of the boy's legs appeared, they were not floating at all but standing barefoot on the broad back of a large draft horse. His legs were gripped by one of the horse trainers sitting astride the giant horse behind him. The man touched his hat.

"Bonjour my friends. Our boy here told us you would be here and in need of assistance," he called. "And ..... here you are."

As they made their way to the village they looked at the back of the boy sitting alone on the giant horse as it pulled. It led the woodworker's horse after having successfully dragged the cart up and over the obstructing hill.

The three men sat on the cart's buckboard seat watching the fields slip by.

"The boy is quite animated," offered Gerard. "Usually he is a shadow. Quiet, shy and little disposed to speaking at all."

The comment was meant as a question. The horseman obliged.

"It was Gregoire. He so wants this apparatus. He feels wondrous new feats of athletic prowess will be possible once his practice mechanism can allay the fears of his trainees. With ropes to provide safety and assuredness they will be unhindered by thoughts of self-preservation and fly to new and amazing heights of ability. Of course you know all of this. After all, you are building the beast."

The man paused and tapped his clay pipe gently on the side of the seat. He shook out the remnants of burnt tobacco and placed the pipe in his shirt pocket.

"When you did not appear this morning with the first part of his beloved project he was quite distraught.

He is a very theatrical man as you know. He saw the worst. You had died. Sold his idea to a rival. Been kidnapped or robbed. Was his machine stolen? So it went. Much wringing of hands was involved.

He was in the arena with all about him offering comfort when he noticed Lucien hovering in the dark edges of the building.

The boy was summoned. Now I have noticed that when young Lucien is wrong with some utterance, it is because a question of such vaguery is put to him and an answer demanded he tends to say anything rather than disappoint the questioner with a refusal or a lack of understanding. It is why the boy has become circumspect. He had lost his confidence."

The man gave a little laugh. He paused as if preparing the best of his narrative.

"It was a thing to behold I tell you now. In his quest for an answer, Gregoire transformed Lucien into a child with belief. We all watched, quite amazed. Perhaps someday there will be a name for abilities such as the boy possesses. Gregoire sat down with the boy, knee to knee. He patted his shoulder and said that if Lucien could answer his question he would be a respected member of the village and all about him would laud his talent and love him for it. Was he willing to help? Lucien looked up, quite bright at all the attention. I mean with all of us standing about watching proceedings. Of course, he would help. Perhaps he trusted Gregoire. Perhaps he knew that a man like Gregoire would not trap him with a question that could not be answered. There was none of his hesitancy, no fear, despite being as yet unaware of what was to be asked. What was the question? He wanted to know.

Ah! It was easy. The boy thought for a second and then replied."

"Your apparatus section is paused by a steep hill halfway on the road to our village. Their horse has not the strength to ascend the grade."

The circus horse man laughed again.

"Gregoire, grabbed him, lifted him up, kissed him on both cheeks and announced that henceforth Lucien should be considered with deference, for he was a hero of the village. People should not be alarmed by his knowing ways. Nor should they pester him with questions the answers to which it would be best they did not know. He, Lucien, would lead the rescue party to a certain victory. As you can see Lucien reacted favourably to this level of trust and it has all worked out quite well. That is the story, my friends. No doubt I will be meeting you on the hill each time you have another piece of Gregoire's machine ready for delivery."

Just then Lucien turned his head and looked at the three men on the cart behind. He smiled happily. His small legs stuck out at an almost horizontal angle from the horse's back as it plodded along. The men nodded and smiled back.

The circus man stopped his cart.

"I'm going to have our little hero returned to his shirt. His shoulders are going pink. Not to spoil the day with too much bravado and sore skin."

Underway once more, one of the men looked puzzled. "Your story is most uplifting. I am happy for the boy. But what if he had been wrong? Gregoire's whole dramatic announcement was based on the boy being correct."

"Ah, as I said, Gregoire is a showman. He is drawn to great drama. Fulfilled by moments of triumph. It is like a strong medicine that he needs to survive. He was caught in the moment. Besides Lucien is seldom wrong. I suspect the theatrical chance outweighed a hint of caution for Gregoire. When we arrive with this huge piece of timber, crafted perfectly by your clever hands, all will be vindicated and we will see another Gregoire performance. Lucien will be reborn all over. I am happy for the boy. Now he will only be asked questions that he can answer. Or wants to answer."

It took a further two months to deliver the sections of Gregoire's machine and piece it together using even larger wooden pegs driven home and glued in position. For added security, the blacksmith placed metal straps and bolts on all the major joints.

Wooden pulleys were fashioned with strong metal pins and tallow was applied to ensure they ran smoothly. Specially made ropes containing sisal, hemp and cotton were delivered. The acrobats were connected to the overhead system via leather and canvas waist girdles that were also strapped between their legs. Each had two ropes connected to looped metal pins on the back of the girdle, ensuring that if in the unlikely event of a rope breakage the second rope would ensure their safety. Even the experienced acrobats were hesitant at first. Despite the girdles holding them steady, they applied no pressure to the apparatus, performing quite simple manoeuvres. Feats that could have taken place with no harness at all.

Gregoire and his assistants worked on their confidence. He challenged them to show strength of character. To be brave and create new and marvellous examples of their work.

After a conference, the acrobats talked then took a most cowardly alternative. They put forward their children to test the equipment.

"They are lighter and more flexible," they explained.

As the collection of smaller acrobats was being fitted to the girdles, Gregoire sidled over to where Lucien sat quietly watching proceedings.

"Will any be harmed?" he whispered from the side of his

mouth.

Lucien looked up at him.

"Non," is all he said.

The children, being children with no fear and a sense
of importance, adapted quickly and began to attempt
spectacular new leaps, somersaults and mid-air rolls.
Their parents, being alarmed and outshone, now hastily
joined in with renewed vigour. Trust in the system and
the men holding their ropes, resulted in some major
improvements in the acts that involved the acrobats.
Gregoire was delighted. All that he had hoped for with his
apparatus was justified.
This village would continue to create gossip and suspicion
regarding its cleverness. Moorant would be pleased.

Lucien still remained a quiet boy but one who was at
peace with his situation. It took several days after his
rescue mission for his sunburn to cool. He announced
that he would henceforth remain inside his shirt.

The lady who believed in Lucien and protected him was
his mother. Her name was Clara. After her drunken wretch
of a husband left the village in the arms of a wanton harlot
when the boy was three years of age, she fed both herself
and the boy with a little work as a seamstress. Her family

had a reputation for masterful embroidery, handed down several generations. While few could afford the finest work, her fair prices made demand quite constant.

The absent husband/father was rarely mentioned until one morning the boy announced that his father was now dead as was the woman in his company. Their chests, he told her were full of water.

She thought little of the information, considering it nothing more than the lively imagination of a young child, until word reached her some weeks later of her husband's demise from falling into a swollen river whilst intoxicated.

Now the child's announcement had credence. It was a singular mystery which the mother put down to some paterfamilias connection. She decided not to speak of the incident in a place full of suspicious gossips.

A month passed and Clara was in conversation with a neighbour. The woman at their small stonewall boundary was distressed at the loss of her expensive brooch. A gift from her late mother. A family heirloom. She tapped her hands to her head in distress. Where could it be? She doubted a theft. Village people were honest. Her family would have to be told.

Lucien looked at the two women. From one to the other. He was intrigued by the topic. Then he clambered up onto

the wall beside the women and hopped down upon the
neighbour's grass. He walked to a foul area where mud
and the rancid milk from the three cows in the shed lay in
a pool. He knelt down and began running his hand about
in the liquid.

"Lucien," his mother scolded. "What are you about? Come
away from there and out of our neighbour's property."
The boy stood and walked to the neighbour. He smiled
and held out his hand.

"Here is your brooch. You dropped it from your blouse
while hurrying to hide that length of cloth from the
merchant in Rue de Couture."
The boy stood without blinking, his hand outstretched,
the brooch gleaming in the dripping milk and mud.
Silence ensued.

Finally the owner of the brooch, her mouth agape said,
"Why thank you, Lucien. You are most kind. What a
wonderful surprise. I am most terribly grateful."
She paused.

"But how ……. came you by such knowledge? A less
charitable woman may think you had a hand in the
disappearance of my broach but you could not have
known of the merchant or my need to keep my purchase
from my husband."
She stared at the boy. Turned her head slightly to better
view the specimen.

It was too much for Clara.

"Take your brooch," she said. " Take your brooch and be thankful. Lucien come here to me now. Come boy right now."

Grasping her son by his clean hand she hefted him back over the wall, bade good day to her neighbour and hurried to her door to take her son inside.
A place of quiet and contemplation and a good number of questions. She feared this event may be one of many to come.
It was.

Then there was the man Gilen Moorant. A native of the village. An illusionist. Not a circus performer, more a trickster of the mind.
As a boy, he enjoyed playing simple tricks to amuse his friends and make a few coins with street performances for visitors. He was known and liked throughout the village.
He had a handsome slightly mysterious look about him. His eyes were dark and hard to catch in any interaction. Traits that suited his calling.
His talents grew and his illusions became quite professional. Larger towns beckoned and his performances gained him an increasing reputation among magic folk and the public.

There was a point, most of the village could name the time even down to the day when it changed. Where Moorant moved on, past the boundaries of clever, well-rehearsed magical enterprise to something none could explain. Where the impossible happened and no amount of acceptance could make the sights that befell his audiences in any way, plausible.

It was here at this time that fate brought forth a quite dramatic shift in the lives of all about, though only in retrospect could this be known.

Moorant gained a celebrity status and thus became desirable. People of note now credited his talent.

So with the level of his incredible performances soon word reached Paris and duly a command was issued for a demonstration of his powers before the President and the Government and many dignitaries. Such requests were not to be ignored as they brought with them obligations to powerful people.

The showing of his craft was to take place at the Palais Garnier especially prepared for the event. Such an honour. A chance to shine.

It is here that the famous man of the village should have recalled a village maxim, ' Position must be balanced by caution.'

A simple dramatic performance would have satisfied the special audience and given the performer a necessary introduction to Paris society. But this was not enough. Gilen Moorant decided to provide an ultimate demonstration of his powers. He would give these notables a performance they would never forget. There would be no path not crossed, impossibility not made possible, no chance of props or sleight of hand just pure unimaginable amazement.

Such was his excitement, to provide the ultimate example of his abilities, he failed to consider that his audience, especially this audience, would not simply walk from the theatre high in praise and quite willing to be satisfied with no further wish of inquiry. These were men and ladies who needed to know all things. Their position in society meant they were in charge at all times. If some event, some action or disturbance took place within their realm then they demanded the right to be all-knowing in matters at hand and decree remedies as seen fit.
It was an inevitable consequence hidden from the performer's mind by a wish to give his audience the very best he could offer. Vanity is a cruel mistress.

Thus, on that night, at the conclusion of the third curtain call at the Palais Garnier the applause faded away as the

President himself stood, straightened his frockcoat and made his way to the stage. Here was a man who lived by his wits and being in charge. Temporarily blinded and at once in awe and grevious concern at what he had just witnessed, he required proof. Answers would be provided and he would be seen by all those assembled as a man who would obtain such answers.

He gave a short speech in which he was fulsome in his admiration of the performance just witnessed.

He freely admitted incredulity at such mastery of the art of deception and granted quite openly that his awe had a hint of concern, that such feats were even possible.

He concluded by pointing out that this is not some barbaric age of the past where feats such as those on this stage tonight would be viewed with suspicion and hints of black arts would be discussed. So, he turned to Gilen Moorant, standing dutifully to the President's left, three paces back, he offered his hand and grasping the man's wrist he held it aloft and stated ...

"Ahh, Monsieur Moorant. We, your audience tonight, are all learned men. While your general people may accept and walk away, we cannot allow that to be the end of the matter. I am sure I speak for all of us when I say that upon a guarantee of myself your President and the assembly here, that no information forthcoming will ever be divulged outside this theatre. I request that you reveal, nay demand, the secret of at least three of your tricks, so that we all may return to our beds this night fully satisfied of your genius and trickery."

A great deal of applause followed while the President continued to smile most graciously and hold Moorant's hand aloft.

When the clamour finally died out and a degree of expectant silence fell across the Palais Garnier, Moorant freed himself from the grasp of the President and slowly stepped forward to the front of the stage, his head bowed. This was a great moment for the head of the French Republic. It would aid his popularity and be a talking point at many a soiree for the coming months.

Gilen Moorant had an ashen aspect to his face. Trapped by his own foolish bravado. What could he have been thinking? To reveal these powers to men who loved and craved power.

Now they sought answers. They felt there was a great deal to be gained by having access to the machinations behind the wonders that had just been witnessed.

Moorant knew the consequences but his choice on that night was to preserve at all costs the truth behind his particular sorcery. When he finally spoke he could hear every word scratching on the papers of his downfall. The nib of the prosecutor's pen delivering sentence by sentence by sentence his inevitable fate.

Moorant did not return to the village. Word came that he was to be transported almost immediately to the penal colonies of the Republic of France in the Pacific Ocean. Most in the village had only a vague idea of how far and where such places were.

To insult the President in front of his cabinet and the most important people in Paris by refusing his request and then explaining that the knowledge the President wished to be divulged was untouchable. How could he dare to say these things, to these people?

He said it was not possible. The knowledge was not his to give. Nor was it safe.

This was not seen as a warning or polite rebuttal but a threat and an astounding act of impudence.

Perhaps though, it was Moorant's final words that night, that sealed his future.

"Monsieur President, perhaps you will understand me when I say that there were no tricks tonight, no sleight of hand, props, trapdoors, mirrors, hidden accomplices or use of light or secret lantern slides. Everything you and your esteemed audience witnessed was real. It was simply 'magic'."

The demise of their talented and mysterious villager

brought about a great deal of sadness and discussions in the main square as to his fate. Matters of interest were generally given a sound working over at the small, endlessly flowing brass water spout that made up the stone feature in the centre. Cleverly the designer of this outlet for fresh, tasty water had made provision for a good number of seats around the feature and under the nearby oak tree so most business of any import took place within its bounds.

For weeks the matter of the demise of Gilen Moorant was the main topic eclipsing all others.

"The man was a genius."

"He was in league with dark forces."

"A very clever magician."

"Too clever perhaps."

"A loss to the village."

"We will not see his face again."

"True. No man returns from these penal settlements."

"The man did not deserve such treatment."

"He was a good man."

They all nodded.

In general terms the memories of Gilen Moorant were favourable. He was well-liked and only a few saw evil in his talents. All agreed he would be greatly missed.

His absence did bring a certain malaise about village life. Until the day, in the early afternoon, when the sun hovered in a blue sky of particular clarity, that the town baker, after making his delivery rounds, wandered up to the group seated about the water trough and said simply, "He's back."

How could this be? The baker was not known for a sense of humour. Quite opposite in fact.
The claim was investigated. Indeed, it seemed to be true.
The man they knew as Moorant was there to be seen.
He sat with a group of the circus folk in their enclave, talking quietly, occasionally moving his hands about to emphasise parts of what he was saying.
Many villagers walked down the slight hill to the large fields where the tents and buildings stood about. They watched Moorant and confirmed to themselves that the man was among them once again. Alive and apparently complete.
At one stage he looked in their direction, smiled and nodded his head quite pleasantly.
They let him be. Just observed.
Yet, it was not Moorant. Certainly not the man they had known only a short time before. He was different. More aged somewhat, careworn, more coloured in his skin.
There was a long thoughtful look in his eyes as if he had been gifted with a view of the world as yet unseen.
Over the following weeks the story of his return, filtered

by many mouths, became known throughout the area. Moorant was back in his village. However, he explained, that he had been away for over four years. Only now could he return.

His choice was to return to a time shortly after his departure. He could now do such things.

Such things? Moving about in time? Arriving and leaving at will. Choosing where and when and what period of life to exist within. Yes, it was all so. Though their man Moorant admitted he knew not why or how or by whose will it was all available. He found it possible and thus he used the powers at his disposal. There were limits he discovered to the ages in which he could traverse but within them, never forward, he was a free agent to make his own decisions. He still worked at refining his skills. This was his 'magic.'

Oddly or perhaps naturally, nobody questioned this possibility. Here was a village of showpeople and their neighbours. If they said it was so then it was so.

It was said he now dwelt in the country of Australia. A place far away from the village and their thoughts. Pursued inland from the coast by French naval personnel he and his companions had crossed the inland ranges to be rid of their tormentors. His band of escapees from the Penal Colony on the Ile de Pins met an inland tribe.

It was at this moment as he greeted the leader of this tribe that he knew he was not alone. His abilities or powers existed in others. It was a moment of exultation. Once free and well settled away from the mountains the task of understanding began. Jarma, the aboriginal man had been in some interactions with the white 'invaders' as he called them. Communication was difficult at first but they found it mutually beneficial to struggle along in English.

The two men learnt to combine their powers and experiment with the consequences. As they refined the skill level they could move themselves and others and their situation about. An example was explained by Moorant. He wished to return to the place the escapees had landed past the reef. To view the scene and ensure that the French Government had abandoned the quest for their capture.

His first attempt landed him on the shore but close to the moment when the frantic retreat of himself and his fellows and their aboriginal friends was taking place.

He watched from afar, keeping out of sight. It was most odd to view himself and the others as they left and headed inland. What would happen if he walked out and greeted himself? It was a lesson for another day.

Refining his use of the skill he managed a week later to arrive once more. His timing was better. The French Navy was departed. Their camp stores and any useful objects were either smashed or confiscated.

He noted with wry amusement that the alcohol the natives had hidden before they left was still intact and stayed hidden. The aboriginal friends were not about but given their nomadic lifestyle and a wish to stay well away from white men with guns he had no doubt they would return at some stage and there would be a celebration and sore heads among the gathering.

The simple trusting people of a rural French village could not understand all the information and ramifications of the tale of Gilen Moorant but their ongoing lack of a need to question such happenings allowed the matter to rest and expand as needed. Acceptance was their nature. Greater minds and greater powers were respected not questioned. Thus their town carried on as it had, with births, deaths, marriages and the annual harvest. Quietly existing and allowing matters to evolve as and when they did.

Moorant dwelt in his old house in the village. Some days he would not be about. It became apparent that he was elsewhere, back at the other place, in northern Australia. Then, there he would be again, walking about, tipping his hat in a most polite and agreeable manner.

His interest seemed now to lie mostly with the circus

people and their camp and buildings. It was a place of learning. A place where they rested between travelling. Where they refined acts, created new acts and worked on their skills. Moorant wanted the best of their talent. He explained that he may have uses for them in his other places. It would be incredibly exciting for them to visit these places and see a world or worlds beyond their own. His suggestions however were not met with excitement or enthusiasm. People were afraid of the concept that they may be transported and transplanted into another place, not of their time.

Until the day an Irishman arrived in their village.

It was mid-morning. He came by the coach. An irregular service that transported people into and out of the village when the horses were capable of handling the roadway. No baggage, just a cloth sack slung across his chest. A flute was visible protruding from a pocket in his waistcoat.

He spoke a little French, enough to be understood. He asked if a man by the name of Gilen Moorant could be found about.

"No," said the villagers. "He was transported to the penal colonies. Such a sad event. We miss him so but alas he has gone from these parts. We doubt we will ever see him again."

The Irishman was puzzled at first by the little he could understand because he knew more than they realised about the special talents of the man he sought.

Then, after sitting in the village square enjoying a drink of their quite fair porter he became aware that he was being watched. Eyes were upon him, conversations were taking place. He suspected, quite correctly, that these fine people were protecting the man Moorant.

How could he explain? Of course, if Moorant were here and authorities became informed of the possibility then they might send an agent, somebody who would be unlikely to be suspicious. Perhaps a traveller from another land would be accepted and the truth revealed.

A degree of diplomacy was in order. Some gesture to confirm his bona fides.

Standing next to his small bench the man from Ireland banged his mug upon the wooden surface. Once all about had become silent and watchful he summoned up the best of his command of the French language

"Mesdames et Messieurs. Je m'appelle Aidan Quinn.

Y a-t-il quelqu'un par ici qui parle la langue anglaise."

A speaker of English?

In the quiet, for some moments, nobody moved then an elderly lady engaged in a noisy discussion with another woman. They carried on their animated exchange until the woman scuttled away. The old lady raised a finger in the direction of Aidan Quinn.

"Momente," she said.

Some minutes passed. The man resumed his seat and his drink. Others in the square returned to their various tasks.

The woman who had been sent away returned. She had a slim, studious looking young man by the elbow, marching him toward their Irish visitor.

When at the bench the young man spoke with a heavy French accent the words, "My name is Hugo. I am a student. I believe you wish to converse with a person in English."

Aidan Quinn smiled and motioned the man to be seated.

"I do that, young Sir. That I do."

He patted the young man's hand which was an Irish habit of reassurance then briefly wondered if a young Frenchman may interpret it otherwise.

"I am on somewhat of a mission and I feel I need to explain to you good people the purpose of my mission. Once I have done that, it is my hope that you will be satisfied as to the safety and propriety of my visit and arrange for me to meet Gilen Moorant.

The Frenchman nodded.

"From what I understand sir you have an interest in meeting a man who no longer resides in this town. You can understand the difficulties of such a request. Still, the people of my village have asked that I give you a fair hearing so that they may understand your interest in our former resident."

Aidan Quinn smiled. He asked for another two ales.

"That is a fair offer. Who knows, when I am finished perhaps you will trust me and Mr Moorant may be found after all."

He raised his eyebrows and smiled.

It took a half-hour. Several times the conversation was stopped while information was passed to the small group that had gathered around the bench. Generally, they shook their heads each time.

With a degree of finality, the student said, "We find your story most compelling. You seem most honourable but we all agree, we cannot produce for you a man who is not here."

Quinn sighed. He stood and raised his hands as if admitting defeat. The crowd made signs of moving away.

"No, no, wait. Please see this," said Aidan Quinn.

He hitched his britches and squared his shoulders.

He walked to a dark area at the side of the inn on the edge of the square. A place where two walls met and formed a hidden corner. It was stacked with wooden boxes for transporting wine.

"Please look here. I am alone. You can see that. Step back now and wait. Give me a moment."

Hugo translated to those who watched.

The Irishman turned and faced into the dark alcove.

Did he in fact vanish?

He seemed to be in conversation with somebody.

"Do not be afraid my dear. I need you for but a moment. Some people would love to hear you sing. To hear your beautiful voice. Please now, step forth me darlin."

There followed a pause. The man reached into the darkness.

He led a young girl out into the square. The crowd gasped. She was so young, so fine of feature. From nowhere she stood before them

Aidan leaned down to the student.

"Could you tell everybody that this is Lucette. She hails from my little town in Ireland. She has a beautiful voice. She would like to sing them a song. A lovely French folksong she knows. When she has finished we would both like to meet Gilen Moorant."

The two men spent three days in earnest conversation. Locked away together in a room at the circus compound, the villagers and even the circus folk could but speculate what amazing exchanges were taking place away from their eyes.

Another man with the abilities of Moorant. What would this mean?

Lucette had performed most beautifully that day in the square. Her diction was excellent, her knowledge of the words exceptional, her voice so pure it brought tears to the eyes of many in the crowd.

They would not let her stop so she sang a lilting Irish melody that brought cheer and smiles to the listeners. She bowed afterwards, nodding her head this way and that to the onlookers. Aidan gave her a kiss on the cheek then whispered to her. He took her hand and led her back to the corner of the inn. And she was gone.

It was here that the young student Hugo said to Aidan, "Sir, it appears that I was mistaken. Gilen Moorant is nearby after all. Would you care to meet him?"

Lucette returned the following day to meet Moorant. Not from the corner of the inn. Some other place unknown. Suddenly she was just there.

Moorant had enough English and Aidan Quinn enough French to make conversation possible.

The boy Lucien was met with the Irish visitors. No doubt his powers were demonstrated and admired. Circus people were involved. Discussions were excited and productive. Now Moorant had a connection with another of his like, the world seemed less puzzling and more wonderful. The village quietly watched. Perhaps they speculated a little.

In the evening they took supper together and included Gregoire in their group. His presence brought an air of great theatrics to proceedings.

Then they were gone. The two Irish folk, Moorant and Lucien. It was all so very odd yet fascinating.

Moorant and Lucien returned the following day.

They had been to Ireland the boy said. For a week.

He enjoyed his visit very much.

Nobody questioned the week or the day, for now. These matters were gone from their ken and thus accepted or not questioned. It was their world now and accepting such things allowed a freedom of thought and the ability to enjoy the moments as they came and went.

The priest of the village when questioned as to God's involvement in these matters was able to point out that all these happenings were of his choosing and no doubt part of some greater plan that we could not understand.

He was happy to see God's infinite wisdom at work in guiding Gilen and the Irishman in their endeavours. The full nature of the journey he would reveal at the day of judgement, which he assured the faithful was quite some time off yet and so not a cause for any alarm.

Most of the village attended church services because they

always had, as had their parents and other generations previous. It was a ritual, a habit. Religion brought no comfort other than that of routine. It did however provide comfort and ritual in times of death and a convenience for the placement of the recently departed.

When told of the priest's thoughts on himself and matters in which he was involved, Moorant smiled and said, "I fear God has been made redundant. We are moving on." Nobody dared repeat such words. So the matter rested.

Within the month word came that people in the town away from the valley were aware that Moorant dwelt once more in the village. Soon they felt gossip or treachery would spread such information too far for safety.
"Then I will be gone," nodded Moorant when told of the situation.
Lucien was consulted and confirmed a visit by some thugs intent on a reward for Moorant's apprehension. They would arrive in two days.
"I will rest tonight then," said Moorant, "and bid farewell in the morn. It is opportune. I should return to the other side of the world. It is in the nature of my journey. It will aid the village. You can laugh in the face of the gossipers and these hunters. Call them out for their foolish belief in silly rumours."

In the first light of the next day, an expectant crowd
gathered on the road near to the circus compound. Under
a group of massive old trees that seemed to provide a
natural stage, Moorant said goodbye to so many people
and friends from the locality.

Among such a lot of heartfelt embraces, he raised his
hands. In the respectful silence, he looked at all these
people before him.

"Please don't be sad. I am not departing from life nor
going on some journey that will take me far away. I will
be quite close and able to return at will. This is simply a
convenience. Plus I should move on to my other village.
The one from which I returned to you. A hub if you will.
They will see me and it will appear I have been gone for
one night only."

Moorant paused as if in thought. Then he looked about at
the crowd one more time.

"Please understand. You saw a different Gilen Moorant
when I returned here. A little older, perhaps wiser.
Each time will be different. It is something I only partly
grasp. A puzzle I have entered. It may be a different
Moorant completely. Revised, reborn, changed but the
essence will be there. Please speak to me each time.
Remind me of who you are and how we are connected.
It will assist the continuance of whatever lies ahead for all

of us. This puzzle we have encountered is for all of us to contemplate and explore."

Gilen Moorant seemed gripped by melancholy. Finally, he stooped and picked up a large canvas bag. He nodded to Gregoire and Lucien and the circus people.

"Keep working. I will have need of you."

He then walked away round the trunk of the nearest tree. When they looked he was gone.

THE IRISH GIRL

She told her mother. Explained that Aidan Quinn
had spoken to her as she walked down the laneway
past the stables, on her way to fetch a jug of milk.
He came from the edge of the whitewashed wall of
the stable. Quite suddenly he was there.
He winked and smiled. Such a nice man, she had
no fear of him despite others of the village being
cautious of his ways.
Would she assist him for a moment? It would be a
great help to him. Some people would like to hear
her sing. Her voice would bring them comfort in a
troubled time.

She glanced from side to side. There were no people. Only Aidan Quinn and herself populated the lane. She would of course be pleased to help. When was this event to take place?

"Oh right now, dear child".

Aidan Quinn, the musician, the man who taught her and encouraged her singing, played his flute so beautifully it made people cry. The man who made her popular throughout the village, stood waiting. He laughed.

"I can see you hesitate. It does involve a little of the oddity about me. The things others are heard to say but do not be afraid my dear. I need you for but a moment. As I said, some people would love to hear you sing. To hear your beautiful voice. You've heard me speak of other lands and other places. Well, I want you to take a deep breath and promise not to cry out. I'll take you there. Please now, step forth my darlin."

He held out his hand.

It was then that Lucette realised she was about to discover the special nature of Mr Quinn's talent. That ability of which he spoke in guarded tones to only a few. Of relocating oneself. She trusted him. He was an honourable man. She took his hand.

Her mother listened to her daughter's story.

Her younger sister sat at their table and tried to understand the conversation, as she ate slices of apple.

"France, you say. A village in France. Just like that."

"Yes, Mother."

"Does Aidan know you're telling me this tale?"

"He does, Mother. He suggested it. He said now he knows he's not alone he would like others to understand."

"I'm not sure I do. Were you afraid child?"

"Momentarily. It is so quick. I was in the lane and then I was in a lovely square in France, in a village, still holding our milk jug and Aidan's hand. I must have looked a little perplexed. The people were most friendly. They smiled a lot. Perhaps as surprised as to what I appeared to be. I received hugs and kisses from quite a number of them once they realised I was a real person and could sing in their language."

Aidan took my milk jug and put it on a table."

"You can pick that up when we return," he said.

I sang the French song Aidan has been teaching me."

Lucette's mother gave a sniff.

"Huh," she said, "I wondered why he felt the need to teach you a song in another language. He's a

trickster our Mr Quinn. Likeable I will admit but ......
There's always something goin' on."
The woman looked about her kitchen.
"And I still do not have my milk. Did you remember
to bring our jug when you returned from this other
land or does it now reside in somebody's parlour in
far-off France?
"I did Mother. I'll fetch your milk right now."
Lucette stood and smoothed down the front of her
dress.
Her mother looked her over. She could not deny
that her firstborn daughter was a beauty. Her
black flowing hair, a complexion of sheer delight,
unblemished soft white with the palest rose in her
cheeks. All enhanced by startling blue eyes. She gets
some of it from me she thought.
Lucette turned at the door.
"Aidan Quinn wishes to pay us a visit tonight, to
speak to you and Father. He would like me to return
to the French village with him to meet a man called
Gilen Moorant. You may all come if you feel I need to
be accompanied and cared for in his presence.
I assume he is asking for your trust."
Lucette's mother stood and placed her hands on her
hips.
"Trust is it," said the woman. "I've never trusted

Aidan Quinn these many years, though I know in my heart he be the most trustworthy man in our village. We'll see what he has to say."

The father of Lucette was a tall man.
Quite intimidating for those who did not know his studious nature and quiet demeanour.
"This tale you tell us Aidan, corroborated by our own daughter, it seems fanciful. Is it not a dream, some fantasy in which you both took part or a tale you passed on to Lucette?"
The man sat at his kitchen table, beside his wife and two daughters. He turned his head slightly as if to show curiosity mixed with a deal of doubt.
"After all you have no proof of such events. How can you simply move from one part of a land to some place in another land? Just so. And in different times. You cannot play with the laws of nature in such a way. What controls and mechanics enable such a feat?"
The man stopped, took a deep breath then continued.
"I've known you many years Aidan, since our days of schooling and in all that time you've proved a fine member of our village. A stout and musically talented chap. You'd make a fine catch for some

lass if you'd put your mind to such things. I am in a
quandary. Where and into what magical, mysterious
place might you propose to take our dear Lucette to
meet some stranger for 'opportunities' as you call
them.? What am I to say? How do I give an answer to
such a plan?"

Aidan Quinn sipped the hot tea from his cup.
"Oh damn that's good," he said to the lady of the
house.
"I appreciate this brew is not a cheap item so I enjoy
it all the more and thank you for it. The French know
nothing of this product".
He turned his face to the man sitting across the
table.
"Now, you sir. Two years ahead of me at school and
one of the brightest pupils. Today the father of this
talented lass."
Aiden paused. He nodded to the little sister by the
fire.
"And perhaps another".
"Let us keep to our oldest for the moment," said the
mother.
Aiden addressed the father once more.
"As you say we have a history. We know each other
well.

How do I accomplish these tasks and how do I
control them? It is a question I put to myself at first.
You should know I was initially quite terrified when
I found these happenings occurring, seemingly at
random, without control. Till I considered their
nature and found that in fact I was causing them
and after further investigation was controlling
their appearance. Learning and understanding the
machinations of the process took time. This man
I wish Lucette to meet has the same powers and
asked the same questions. In response I can only ask
you, do you make your heart beat, do you instruct
your lungs to expand to take in new air? These
things take place without your conscious effort. So
it is with me and the man Moorant.
It seems the power we possess enables us the ability
to move, to adjust and to choose time as we desire.
It does not falter and is never wrong. Why this is
possible I do not know. Do we control it or does it
control us? That I cannot answer. Are there laws
and limitations? I suspect there are many. I can only
discover such things by using the abilities and
seeking the edges of the whole."
Aidan stopped, staring down at his large cup of tea.
He ran his finger around the rim. Took another sip.
He looked about the room his brows knitted as if

pondering a way forward. Finally, he looked up at his adversary in the form of Lucette's father.

"It is not fair," he said, "You deserve more information so that your mind is clear. Would you come with me for a brief walk? Our village is pleasant this time of year. While I wish no disrespect to your lovely wife, there are times when menfolk need to go into great detail so as to understand each other. Let's enjoy the fresh night air while I discuss with you this proposal all round, with that greater detail, so that you may see my actions are true."

A silence fell across the room after the two men departed closing the door quietly behind them. Lucette's little sister sat still by the hearth, her eyes moving in expectation from Lucette to her mother. The house lamp and candles flickered painting distorted shadows on the white walls. Finally, it was the woman who broke the silence. She looked at her eldest daughter. It was a statement more than a question.

"Special men's business indeed. He's going to take him there isn't he."

Lucette looked at her mother and nodded slowly.

"I suspect that is his intent, Mother."

Lucette was away from her parents for two days.
Two real days as it happened. Despite their
acceptance of the wondrous abilities of Aidan
Quinn and their trust in him, they were relieved
when Lucette entered their house once more. Her
countenance was one of content. She had so much
to tell her parents.

Meetings with circus folk, entertainers, animal
trainers, acrobats and more. The man Moorant, the
magician, was indeed a talented, clever man of, she
imagined, great power.

There was a boy Lucien who had visions of the
future and the past. She talked with him for some
time. He seemed like a brother.

Some speculation occurred regarding their names.
Could the closeness of Lucette and Lucien be just
a coincidence or were greater forces at play? Their
mannerisms, their very appearances seemed related.
Gregorie the head of the circus and a man of much
excitement and vigour suggested to Lucette that
she travel with his troupe billed as 'The Irish
Nightingale'. This did not appeal but thankfully
Aidan was able to tactfully extract her from the
suggestion with information regarding her sick
mother.

"And what, pray tell me child, is the ailment that afflicts me?" asked the mother of Lucette. "I have been used in a subterfuge it seems."

Lucette's father visited once more with Aidan and requested that he be allowed to simply wander about the area. People took note of him and were polite with a "Bonjour" or "Salut" but left him to conduct his ramblings.

The villagers had grown used to these Irish people just appearing. Aiden's initial caution of seeming to arrive by coach was not necessary.

The man returned with a mission in mind.

"I have always had an urge to master another language. There seemed little point until now with no one in the area with whom I could converse."

He took Aidan's elbow as they walked back to the man's house.

"I would not wish to impose or put you in any discomfort but I would consider it a kindly act if you were to take me to the French village whenever you can so that I might enjoy the company of people of a foreign land. It would be fascinating."

Aidan Quinn looked at the man's eager face.

"If having you fascinated is pleasing then I will so oblige."

Only a day after her return, the girl stood in the centre of Aidan Quinn's parlour.

With her hands clasped daintily at her waist, she concentrated on holding a perfect pitch as her teacher tapped the keys of a small piano. Next to the piano was a large jardiniere on a stand. A purchase made by Aidan while in his French village. It formed a barrier between the man and his pupil. Thus her teacher had to lean back in order to look at Lucette. His face would appear and disappear as he struck chords and then checked the results. Lucette was amused but she could only admire his enthusiasm and dedication. Her training had increased. She did not mind. Singing was her joy. However, there was a reason for the activity.

Aidan spoke of a major event. It was destined to happen and she would play her small part in the proceedings.

On a stage in front of an audience. She would be acclaimed by the people who saw her.

It was all at the behest of Gilen Moorant. A major coming together of much talent with a purpose of making contact with an audience.

The detail and exact purpose of the show were not divulged but Lucette was quite excited by the prospect of having a large number of people hear her sing.

Aidan was especially conscious of giving the girl greater vocal power, to project her voice and overcome a theatre size area.

Even her entry onto the stage was to be rehearsed with Moorant. Each part of the proceedings was to appear natural and have a slightly unplanned or casual note to the act.

It was, Aidan explained, to give the impression of great power in which Moorant could summon events at will.

This theatre will be at a time that is yet to come for us and so will have mechanical and electrical devices that will need to be commandeered, apparently by magic.

"It is," Aidan explained, "the art of illusion."

He winked.

"We have a great advantage over performers who rely solely on their immediate surroundings but stagecraft must still be employed to its utmost to ensure a fine performance."

THE MAGIC

Large cities have them. Known and respected but always on the fringe. It's what they're called. They never seem to break into the mainstream of the entertainment industry. It is because the 'industry' is run by PR people and accountants. It is a profit-driven factory specifically geared to charging a great deal of money for tickets and moving massive numbers of people into massive venues.

Small venues in old buildings in unfashionable areas struggle to create interest, struggle to pay expenses and never gain enough oxygen to have themselves noticed.

It is the way of the world. Yet there are always a select few who take on the challenge. They own the places, rent the places, paint scenery, keep the sound going and the curtain rails oiled, man the ticket booth, do the books, speak to the fire safety people, perhaps act in the first scene then reappear at intermission behind the small bar. Then there are the patrons. Those who are not involved in the running of the venue, will often be of a charitable frame of mind, see themselves as patrons or just like seeking out the obscure, often bad, sometimes very good performances in the subworld of small theatres.

They may hear of something special happening at a place they know. Word will get around. A local newsletter will alert them to one last week of the excellent play by a local writer which has been favourably received by those who attended the performances in the previous week.

They will be warned that this will be their only chance to experience the wonderful inventiveness of the play and the performance.

The hint will be that the whole thing is destined for greater glory but the length of the play's run as in most cases, will be down to the very slim takings at the door and the need to pay the costs and move onto something, anything that will bring in more cash. Sadly and probably, a bad, tasteless gig by somebody outrageous enough to draw a crowd of the less discerning of potential customers. Perhaps even one of those dreadful 'tribute' acts who ply their trade by pretending to be somebody famous.

The place I have in mind was such a venue and it was this very problem that confronted the owner when he saw the last of the twenty-two members of his audience out the door on a Friday night in winter.

The colder months were worse. His building had to be heated to save the attendees from shivering in their seats.

If the house was full then body heat did most of the work and the heating could be minimal. It was one of those win/win things that happened rarely.

Tonight the play, a comedy with a strong social message, had gone well. The audience laughed and cried and had been swept along by the enthusiasm of the playwright and main character. His small cast all put in delightful, confident performances. They could not be faulted. The girl who played his love interest had such an unusual and pretty face combined with a rare sense of timing that he felt she was destined for a bright future.

Beyond all this feeling of goodwill and sense of accomplishment stood the hard reality of outgoings versus income.

He closed and locked the front doors, then helped Annie who ran the whole foyer area with a quick clean up before seeing her out the side entrance, then he turned off the outside and foyer lights. There was no point avoiding or putting off his next duty. He walked slowly and thoughtfully down the aisle, past the empty seats and made his way along the stage front and up the stairs at the side. Once through the door into the land behind the curtain, he worked his way past the darkened props, ropes and the stage machinery console toward the green room. He could see the light coming out under the door. They would all be in there, cleaning off makeup, getting changed. Their mood would be mixed. Exhilarated at their sterling performance but aware, one and all, that the week's box office had started okay then dived to unsustainable depths. How charitable the owner was prepared to be was unknown. They were due to run for three more weeks. He could hear them talking.

When he opened the door they seemed to know.

This particular theatre was an inheritance type.
Some venues are bought and refurbished by starry-
eyed people with hopes and little future. Others
are reinvented by money-men who can see a quick
profit in a niche market. There are a fair few tired,
desperate old buildings run by enthusiastic co-ops
who keep alive by using friends and neighbours as
their source of labour and audience.
The owner of this theatre had spent his childhood
in this very place. He grew to love the theatre
people. It was quite successful and times were
good. Perhaps the French heritage of the owners
gave the place a little foreign chic. The building was
well maintained and nearly always full of satisfied
patrons.
The boy knew every inch of the establishment.
He did many jobs involved in the theatre's function
and productions. His sister was less involved.
The world is ever evolving. The day came when his
father, who had smoked far too many Gauloise over
the years, called his children into his study and
talked to them for some time.
It was to do with his Will. When they had finished
it was determined that the son would take over
the running of the theatre and the daughter would

receive a handsome amount to pursue her interest in
anthropology.
Both parents were gone from their lives within three
years.

In quieter moments the man reflected that he was
gladdened by his parent's relatively early departure
from life thus sparing them being witness to the
decline of the place they held so dear.

On Monday, two days after paying out and
dismissing the young playwright and his cast, it was
time to contact his insurance.
All theatre people know of the 'insurance'. It is the
act or play or performer you have on standby. The
one who you have spoken to and shaken hands
with regarding a possible spot in your theatre.
A potential lifesaver. The contract is verbal but
sacred. Or it was once.

"Leon. Hullo, my man. Hope you're fit and well.
Listen, I won't hold you up. I've got some great
news. I've found you a spot. When I said I'm looking
out for you I really meant it. That handshake
agreement. It's my word. Had to work on it but we
can get it all happening next week. Sooner if you

like. Open this Friday. Get some publicity happening. You're becoming a bit of a celeb. It should be great."

It seems Leon was convinced that because of his recent climb up one or two rungs of the ladder of fame he was deserving of greater things. Without asking for permission to walk away from his handshake he was already involved in some other project that he felt was "more suited to his considerable talents".

Now the man sat in the theatre's office and mulled over his predicament. Three weeks to fill. An expensive, potentially disastrous hole. The next people on the billing could not come sooner. He was at a loss. Anybody worth having on the stage, anybody who could pull in an audience was not to be found.

So, a theatrical moment was needed. One of those precious events that occur regularly in b-grade romantic dramas but never in reality.

Yet, it was here that what he would later call 'the magic' happened.

While telling himself that drinking whiskey daytime and nighttime was a dangerous path to enter, he heard a precise knock at his office door. As usual, he always locked the outer door of the theatre when he entered his building, so nobody could be there.

Until the knock came again.

Concerned for his safety he opened his door with some hesitation. A figure stood there. Upright and calm. There did not seem to be a threat.

"How did you get in here?" he asked the man.

The man was quite tall in a sinuous way and had an annoying benign smile. He had a slightly dark complexion.

"Magic," he said, with a little flourish of his hand. It was never ascertained whether his caller was revealing what method he used to get through the locked door or simply announcing a subject he wished to discuss. Still, he did not appear dangerous. Something that must always be considered when greeting a stranger alone, in the back of an empty theatre. In balance, this was the world of oddities. Most involved in this business were aware of the whole world being a stage.

"I wish to avail you of my services."

"Your services?"

"I deal in magic."

"You're a magician."

"I deal in magic."

They still stood at the office door.

"May I come in? I will explain."

Seated across the desk from the theatre owner, the man began to talk.

"I chose your theatre because it suits my requirements. You will be amply rewarded with full houses every night of my time with you. I wish to start on Friday night. It will be best to ease the patrons into the magic."

The theatre man was quite amused by his visitor's chutzpah but it was time to interrupt.

"Excuse me. I didn't get your name."

"Moorant."

"Well Moorant, I know nothing about you but what I can tell you is that I just let go of a group of highly talented actors performing a great play. Reason, despite the obvious quality of the whole production, it was not attracting an audience. So you see, replacing these highly talented people who could not attract an audience with a 'magician' is not going to solve my problem. It will exacerbate it."

"I am not a magician. I deal in magic."

"And you've filled theatres throughout the known world?"

"No, I have not performed for some time. It needed to be prepared. Tamed if you like. Now it is ready."

The banter continued for more minutes. Each thrust and parry was met and returned in equal measure. Finally, the theatre man delivered his coup de grace. The well-worn phrasing that could be employed at any time to dissuade a problem 'talent' from pursuing their self-promotion any further.

"Well, it is pity you do not have your props with you so that I could judge your performance and give an opinion. A shame really but my time is rather precious so I'll say good day and ...."

"Oh, of course, it is the least I can do. A small sample for you, to allay your fears. If you would care to accompany me to the stage area I will put your concerns to rest."

It was perhaps the whispered but overpowering nature of the man's voice that annoyed the theatre owner the most.

He was a reasonable man. He would indulge this strange chap, be unimpressed by some tired old tricks and graciously show him out the door. The door he was sure he had locked.

Placed in the centre about four rows back from the front the man watched his visitor disappear up the stairs at the side of the stage.

He waited for the man to appear on the stage.
Instead, the man was beside him or actually behind
him. He leaned over and spoke.
"I forgot to inform you of my requirements."
It was unnerving. How had he managed to get from
the side of the stage to a position behind him? That
was impressive at least.
"I ask that you do not move from this seat under any
circumstances. Do not cry out and do not be afraid."
The theatre owner turned to speak but there was no
one there. He had wanted to mention that he had
heard such theatrical nonsense before, however, he
would abide by the rules.
Stage lights blinked on and the visitor, who said he
did 'magic' was standing in the centre bathed in a
blue spotlight.
He could operate stage lights? The audio/lighting
desk was at the back of the theatre. Once there had
been a sound engineer, nowadays it was a set and
forget operation.

The man on the stage began.
"You will forgive me if I lack a little fluidity at first.
My last performance was in Paris some time ago. It
was a triumph but there were consequences."
Moorant then raised his hands and held them out to

the side.

"Let us begin".

He half turned.

"Lucette, would you come forward and render a song for the gentleman."

A petite girl of about ten or eleven walked from the back of the stage. She must have been cleverly hidden in the shadows.

She was quite pretty with dark shoulder-length hair held by a black band and deep blue eyes. Her dress was full and old-fashioned. Tied at the neck with a velvet bow. In front was a little white apron. Her boots were buttoned up past her ankles.

She looked up at the man.

"What shall I sing?" She had an Irish lilt in her voice.

"Oh I think you know," the man said.

The girl smiled.

"Very well."

Music began to play. Yet the kill switch on the PA was definitely locked off.

The girl moved to the front of the stage, clasped her hands in front of her sweet dress and looked straight at the theatre owner.

Moorant spoke.

"Let's pretend that Lucette is from the new colony of

Sydney town. Now this song would normally be sung by a young man but it's such a pleasant tune I'm sure you'll make allowances."

She began to sing with a beautiful clear strong voice.

"In a neat little town, they called Belfast
Apprentice to trade I was bound
And many an hour's .... "

The audience of one felt quite odd. He heard his mother's voice as she sang her favourite song to him. The chorus stirred such memories in him.

"Her eyes they shone like diamonds
He thought her the queen of the land
And her hair, it hung over her shoulder
Tied up with a black velvet band"

As the song ended and the music faded a boy of about twelve and a man skipped past down the aisle. They leapt spectacularly up onto the stage. They were alone. The girl was gone. Moorant was gone. The two on stage moved forward and winked at their audience. Their costumes were of another century. Tight-fitting Britches shirts and waistcoats. Exceedingly handsome, possibly father and son. Slicked back hair. The man had a thin pencil moustache. They bowed and then for the next ten

minutes performed acrobatic feats that were quite
insane and impossible as the boy was hurled up
out of sight, bent, twisted and contorted yet always
returned to the safety of the man's arms. All while
a drum and fife played vigorously. Then they were
gone. Or did he hear them run past, back up the
aisle?

The magic man was back in the spotlight. By some
trick of light, another man stood suddenly beside
him. This new person looked unkempt and wild. He
wore a long black coat to just past his knees. His hat
was a wide-brimmed black affair pulled low over his
eyes. His beard was dark and tangled.
The only colour about the man was the obvious gold
hilt of a knife sticking from the man's waist belt. He
seemed huge and deranged.
"What shall I do?"
The man, the conjuror, whatever he was, replied in a
loud husky voice.
"Something dangerous."
The man in black lowered his head and turned it
to one side as if attempting to mask his action of
removing the knife from his belt. He stayed bent
with his head down. He could be heard growling,
muttering curses and angry words. He seemed to be

speaking an odd type of French.

The audience of one was fearful. This visitor had a veritable human menagerie hidden in his theatre. How he had secreted them about the place was a mystery. Now it seemed to be going too far.

The man in black suddenly roared. He raised himself to his full height, then stormed to the front of the stage.

He pointed at the man in the seat. His eyes were crazed. This was not acting! He was a lunatic, yelling threats and barbarous taunts.

His arm went up and with a terrifying precision he launched the giant, gold-handled dagger straight forward.

Trapped, locked by horror the theatre owner could only lean back, eyes wide and wait for the glinting blade to bury itself in his chest.

The theatre lights came on. Moorant was alone on the stage bathed in a dazzling white spotlight. He raised his hands as if in humble acceptance of applause then performed a sweeping bow.

He walked forward.

"Excuse my last performer. Gregoirie is an exceptionally fine actor you must agree."

He paused. Tilted his head.

"That was a little of the magic."

Looking wildly about, shaking and sweating the theatre owner, twisted in his seat trying to see every corner of his domain.

"I am rather angry," he said, at last, hoping his voice did not tremble. "Bringing a whole range of people into my establishment without permission. How long were you here setting up this trickery? Playing about with sound and light systems ...."

The man was no longer on the stage. Now he was seated next to the theatre owner who jumped involuntarily.

"I assure you, sir, I am the only person here. I was always the only person here. I entered your premises for the first time moments before I knocked on your door. As I said, I do magic."

The Friday opening night was quiet. Though upon inspection the theatre's seats were half full with one-half hour to go.

The theatre owner did not know what purpose he served anymore. He arrived at 6pm expecting his performer to be waiting, perhaps with a truck full of props and assistants. Nobody awaited him. He panicked for a while until, as he hovered backstage.

then the man was suddenly there.

"Do you need a hand with any equipment?"

The performer seemed amused, though it was hard
to tell.

"I am prepared. I have all I need. I spoke to the
delightful lady in your foyer. The one who sells
tickets, answers the phone, takes bookings and
handles the refreshments bar. I purchased a bottle
of mineral water. I will place it on a stool at the side
of the stage. My voice occasionally becomes hoarse
and requires lubrication."

"So you're completely ready?"

"Yes. I will wait until the theatre is quite full.
Running a little late will build some tension."

"Well, not too late. I doubt the theatre will reach
anywhere near capacity."

"I will sit alone now and prepare my thoughts."

The man walked across to a lounge chair prop
at the very back of the area. He was dressed in a
well-fitting suit and tie giving the impression of a
company executive. Though his dark demeanour
spoke of a deeper purpose.

He lowered himself gently into the cushion seat,
placed his arms on the high sides and closed his
eyes.

After the 'sample' performance at the beginning
of the week, the owner and the performer had
adjourned to the theatre office.

The owner decided he had been in the hands of an
exceptional hypnotist. The whole performance had
taken place in his mind controlled and conducted by
the man on the stage.

He accused the man of hypnotism.

The man simply replied, "I do magic. Your mind was
untouched."

Normally the theatre owner would not consider
such an act for his establishment but he was rather
desperate.

He was also concerned about the mental health of
his odd potential performer. Still, he pressed on.

"I can't pay a lot. This place does not make great
profits."

The man leaned back in his chair.

"Can I make you a proposal? One that may allay your
concerns of monetary embarrassment. I will ask for
20% of each ticket you sell. That way you will have
no burdensome contract or obligation and I will be
responsible for my destiny.

My only other condition is that you double your
normal admission price. I offer my hand to shake as

a binding token of faith and goodwill on both our parts."

After the man had departed the theatre owner sat at his desk for quite some time, unable to access any logic in the fact that he had indeed shaken the man's hand and with little or no idea what 'performance' he had invested in he could only hope it would not be an embarrassing failure.

Being a professional he created some strong red and black posters announcing the limited availability and performance by ……… It was here that he realised he had forgotten the man's name and he had no method of making contact.
So his new act became 'A Man of Magic' - the like of which you have not witnessed nor will ever see again.
He booked some short commercials on local radio and sent out a press release in the hope that one of the dailies might have a quiet day and run the piece. He did double the admission price, When he checked with Annie mid-week she informed him that there was a steady flow of bookings.

At five minutes to curtain time, he rang Annie.

"I've closed the ticket booth," she said. "We're full. I swear half the people have no idea why they're here. Just concentrating on looking after the bar. Not sure we've got enough booze. Does your Mr Magic have an intermission?"

"I've no idea."

The performer was still seated in the armchair. He opened his eyes as the owner approached.

"Time to do your stuff, my friend."

The man raised his hand.

"Five minutes over. It adds expectation."

"Any special lighting you want? Sound? A little bit of reverb or echo on the mike?"

"None of that will be necessary. All is in hand. It would please me if you took a chair out to the aisle at the side and just enjoyed my magic."

There was indeed a short intermission.

The audience mingled in the foyer. They purchased wine and spirits from Annie who rushed to serve their requests before the time was up.

The owner stood to one side and listened to the conversations taking place around him. Some mentioned the amazing foursome who threw balls of light about the stage in a dazzling display. Others

thought the man who managed to hurl two small
children, a boy and a girl, into the air one after the
other as they completed intricate acrobatic feats
was quite astounding. Then there was the box from
which the man produced an array of people and
animals and created a small village scene before it
all went dark and the village was replaced by sand
and ocean and large seabirds swooping over the
audience. The man caught a fish.
A squirming, thrashing fish. He fed it to a cormorant.
And the beautiful voice of that beautiful French lady
as she sang Ave Maria.
The owner listened and absorbed their delight and
enthusiasm for what they had obviously witnessed.
From his seat in the side aisle, the owner had
also watched the performance. It consisted of the
performer walking about on stage and talking to the
audience. He announced the acts and the audience
saw the show. This, he continued to do until
announcing intermission.
Whatever took place in his theatre it could be seen
only by those in the paying seats.
At least he knew the man's name once more.
He announced himself before his performance.
People were now filing back in for the second half of
the show. He stood and wondered what new delights

they were now going to be fooled into thinking they were seeing.

Moorant was at his side. Once again as if from nowhere. How did he do that?

"You feel cheated?"

"It's all an illusion. I see that now. Haven't figured out how. What tricks you use to make it happen." Moorant answered in that silvery voice.

"Oh, I assure you. None of it is an illusion. I simply kept the viewing area to the seats in front. It is happening. It is simply magic."

He paused then placed his hand on the owner's arm.

"I have a seat for you. It is 4H on the centre aisle. Please sit there now. It will bring you in. Do not move."

Then annoyingly he was gone.

The owner looked out through the curtains. The audience had all returned to their seats and waited expectantly.

He could see that 4H was vacant. As he was about to move, Annie appeared beside him looking in.

"He is truly amazing," she said. "I've been watching at the back. Where did you find him?"

The lights went dim, then completely out. The

theatre was in darkness. The audience's heart rates increased as did their breathing.

A small glow appeared on stage. Moorant could be seen standing near the glowing point.

A child's voice said, " I can see it. It is faint."

"Walk toward it. As it grows stronger it will show you the way."

"Can I trust you, Monsieur Moorant?"

"Nothing will harm you. I will take care of you. These people are waiting to meet you. Your English is very good."

It was here that the owner realised the voice had a heavy French accent.

Then he appeared. The audience gasped. It was as if the figure had stepped through a hole. He looked ten or eleven. He wore a white blouson shirt and knee britches. He had bare feet and seemed pale. His hair had dark brown curls and his eyes were dark.

He stood next to Moorant and gently smiled as he looked up at the man. Moorant in turn put his arm around the boy's shoulders as if to reassure him.

"This is Lucien," he announced. "He is here to answer your questions. Any question? Please put your questions to my young friend and he will provide the answer. If an answer is possible."

For some seconds the audience was mute, then a woman's voice came from the back of the theatre.

"Where are you from, Lucien."

The boy looked confused.

"From .... back there. From my village" He pointed behind, over his shoulder.

Before the answer could be pursued a man called out.

"When will I die?"

The boy looked up at Moorant. The man shrugged.

"He wants to know."

"At five minutes past four o'clock in the afternoon on the 20th day of August."

The man stood.

"August is next month. What year."

"This year."

A groan swept through the audience.

"He's only joking," somebody said. Still the questioner was quite deflated.

"Will my daughter marry?"

"Yes, to a man called Albert. They will have twin girls and call them Alexandra and Lily."

"How do you know the future?"

"It is all there. If I look."

"Where is my house key that I lost?"

"It is in the mud by the lake in the park where you

walk with your dog."

"Why should we believe you?"

Moorant answered.

"There is no need. Make your choice. Perhaps this is all just trickery. A bit of silly fun. Quickly forgotten. It is for you to judge."

The banter and questions continued in a lighthearted way for almost another ten minutes. The theatre owner noted that the boy did not have the slightest hint of bravado or theatricality about him. He answered the questions confidently and quickly but in a manner of somebody who believed all that he said and found the process quite natural. A man asked if he could have the winning numbers for the Grand Golden Casket draw that was to take place in one week. The boy quickly gave ten numbers. Such was the amused atmosphere in the theatre that nobody bothered to take note. Then came the moment when a very plump, middle-aged woman in the very front row rose from her seat and announced that this beautiful young boy was obviously tired and needed rest. She held out her arms toward the stage.

"Lucien my dear. I'm a mother. You seem such a sweet child. But I can feel you've been here long enough. You've given us all a lot of enjoyment this evening with your performance. I'd like to give you a great big hug before you return to your ……. ha 'village'."

She made toward the steps that led to the stage.

"Madam!" Moorant snarled as he held the boy away and behind his body.

"Return to your seat at once. Nobody should ever approach or touch my performers."

His voice was loud and determined. The woman looked startled and stumbled back to her seat. Moorant meanwhile walked the boy Lucien backwards on the stage. He allowed him to stop briefly and give a polite half bow to the audience then Moorant was alone on the stage.

He came forward and also gave a slight bow.

"That concludes tonight's activities. You may leave now."

The theatre lights came on and the stage was empty. The magic had stopped.

The following night the young girl who had appeared in Moorant's 'sample' arrived on the stage once again.

She sang an American traditional song.

"Come, come angel band.

Come and around me stand.
Bear me away on your snow-white wings
To my immortal home."
Her accent this time sounded southern American
though he was not sure whether it was false.
Perhaps it was Irish after all.
Many other delights followed. The house was full
once more.
An Irishman called Aidan played his flute with
such beauty and melancholy that some audience
members were brought to tears.
The theatre man watched. There were clues he
thought. These performers were all of a similar
demeanour, had similar physical features, were
dressed in Olde World garb and looked a little lost.
Despite their amazing efforts, he thought they
were confused. Were they captive or coerced? Or
possibly just nervous, as if the experience was quite
frightening.

At the end of the first week, he did not take his
seat. Instead, he waited at the back of the stage
watching the man Moorant alone on stage showing
his audience 'magic' that only they could see.

At the conclusion of the show, before the performer

could disappear the theatre man confronted him and laid a hand on his arm.

"I'm a curious man, he said, "I know, I should just accept your talents and enjoy the exceptional income. But I need some answers."

"No, you don't. They're not answers I can give. I was born and I knew."

"What did you know?"

"That I was a magic man."

"There are others like you?"

"The stories say so."

"Whose stories? Where are you from? I can't safely pick your nationality."

Moorant smiled gently.

"I am from here and elsewhere. I did not arrive. We have been here for many centuries."

The theatre owner was silent while he thought about the answer.

"You're native? You're first nation? Your accent is French at least."

"In part. A little".

"Perhaps I understand. A Kurdaitcha man?"

"That's just a name. There are many names in history for people with possible talents. Where we are and what circumstances surround us determine our position in society."

Moorant waited patiently for the next question.

It did not come so he spoke.

"Tomorrow night will be my final performance.

All the audience who had to come will be exhausted by then. They will be a large group these last ones. You can pay me all that I am owed."

The theatre owner was shocked.

"Well, yes, of course. The funds are there for you ..... Look, I know this was a loose arrangement but please reconsider. We're going so well. Could you extend for perhaps another week at least?"

"I am sorry," said Moorant, "I have seen all that I needed to see here. The message is out. The seeds have been cast. There is now a reason for me back at my place and no further reason to stay".

While the conversation continued for some minutes and various proposals were suggested for an extension of the run, it came to nothing. Moorant was to leave.

The final night was different. People stood in the aisles from the front to the rear. Some sat in area before the stage. No space was spared.

At ten minutes past curtain up time, the house lights dimmed.

The theatre man had secured himself a centre seat

two rows back for this performance. He had been assured all those present would be able to see the show.

For a short time, the darkness prevailed until the audience grew silent and respectful.

It began with a substantial fire burning in the centre of the stage. Normally such a sight would cause chaos in a theatre as patrons rushed and pushed for the exits.

No person moved.

A didgeridoo began to drone, pulsing and throbbing, becoming louder. It set the mood. Then it stopped and a warrior walked out and sat cross-legged in front of the fire facing the audience.

He looked about the people for a while as if memorising all the faces, and then he spoke.

"There is a tree, an old tree, dead many years and yet alive to my place. It is the marker. It is the place where the crossover takes you in and the magic begins. You cannot go. You people are not welcome. Tonight I will take you there. It is a glimpse. A gift for you."

The light became brighter. The stage was now a lake. A stretch of immense sparkling water that looked so peaceful and alluring. Sitting on the shore with his toes supporting his didg was a boy of about ten.

Dressed in a simple loincloth. It was not entirely sure that he was even native. He played a quiet breathy rumbling sound. It floated in the hushed theatre like some unearthly creature. Then he stopped. He stood and looked at the audience. His chest, legs and face were painted with white streaks. He began to dance, shuffling his feet on the white sand of the shore.

He circled as he danced bowing down with his arms out, like a bird of prey watching the ground. Now the boy was in a jungle clearing. Still, he danced. Two girls could be seen sitting in the undergrowth beating short sticks in overlaying time.

The dance stopped abruptly. The boy and the two girls walked along a path, pushing glistening palm fronds aside as they went. They emerged into a huge open area of grass and trees. It was partially shaded by what seemed to be a massive rock overhang. There were strange dwellings built of stone with timber balconies, also gardens of what appeared to be vegetables and fruit.

The theatre owner remembered thinking that Moorant was going too far with this Hollywood fantasy place.

It looked like a representation of some Shangrila in a movie. Except that it seemed so real. Still, he felt an underlying sense of peace that belied his cynicism.

The young warrior appeared again. Many adults and children gathered around him. The didgeridoo and click sticks started up again. They all danced and swayed as the music or sound became louder. They were chanting. It became a roar. A deafening, chilling, rumble of massive, overwhelming sound and strength. The power was terrifying. Then it was gone.

In the darkness, members of the audience could be heard making odd noises, coughing and breathing fast.

Moorant appeared on the empty stage in a single spotlight.

He waited.

When all was silent he spoke in those deep tones he employed.

"You have visited ..... my place."

An audience member called out.

"It doesn't exist, does it? I mean it was all an illusion. We'd know, wouldn't we? If it was there, somewhere."

"How could such a place exist." Mooorant held out his hands. "As you say, it would be known."

Another man spoke.

"Those people were aboriginals or pretending to be

aboriginals. There seems to be a mix of cultures."

'Perhaps you are right," said Moorant.

He gave a deep theatrical bow and was gone.

Drums began and two men with long waxed moustaches and a woman, all with colourful tights and tops, twirled and danced and juggled amazing things as they swept about the stage.

Two other acts followed, straight from Moorants stable of strange old circus-like performances. Some very odd crazy clowns and then a man with a bear and a monkey who danced and skipped as the man played a small accordion.

At their conclusion as they abruptly took one step back and vanished.

Moorant appeared again. He held up his hands to silence the applause.

"Thank you for visiting and thank you for your patronage. There will be no more. You may go now."

People called from the audience.

"Explain how this all happens".

"We need to know".

"How do you make us all believe what we see?"

Moorant answered in a benevolent tone.

"It is all magic. Nothing more. If you wish to believe, then call it sleight of hand."

The spotlight went to black. He was gone.

In the theatre office twenty minutes later the owner and the performer shook hands. As requested the payment was made in cash in a cotton bag.

"That's quite a lot of money. Will you be safe?"

"Yes, I will be completely safe. It was good of you to ask."

"Can I visit your place?"

"No."

"Why did you tell the audience they were not welcome?"

Moorant paused.

"It is human nature. To want something you are told you cannot have."

ARTIE

It began with a sigh. Quite soft, through the hedge.
A thick green side barrier to my neighbour.
The day was warm. It had promise. There were uncared-
for tools in the shed, together with a lawnmower that
looked dangerous as well as inoperative.

But first, why I am here?
When you're young you can conquer any obstacle.
Though naivety appeared to be my Achilles heel. The
agent was persuasive.
"The gentleman wishes that the modest garden be
brought back to a semblance of its former delightful

outlook. If this small task is completed to his satisfaction
then the rent you are agreeing to pay will be reduced
by twenty-five percent and will remain at what I must
say is already a generously low rate whilst ever the
garden is maintained in an orderly and pleasing fashion.
Certain additions to the garden will be, from time to time,
introduced and you will be required to install said items at
a handsome fee to be negotiated as and when such events
occur."

I have been here for a week. It has rained for a week.
Today it is dry and sunny. Winter is ending. Spring is
making an effort to establish itself on the landscape.
When I viewed the property with the agent it was also
raining heavily so the garden received only a cursory
glance. I now see it is much bigger and more complex than
I realised. There is also another section of the garden at
the back.
Viewed from this front yard the building is quite
magnificent. A large two-story white rendered Victorian
beast. (Three-story if I count the basement.) A sort of fat
detached inner city version of a terrace house. It has a
high front wall with an iron gate and a path that leads to
three wide handsome marble steps to a wide tiled landing
and a hefty front door. The door has a large brass knocker.
The upper level has a wide balcony with French doors.

When first built the view was probably quite extensive.
Now the view is mostly obscured by trees in the garden
and the garden of the neighbour wherein stands an
identical house to this one.
"Why are you showing me this property?" I asked. "It's
delightful. It would be perfect but the rent is obviously
more than I could afford."
"I'm showing this property because you can afford it."
"How is that?"
"My client, the owner, has special requirements. You suit
those requirements."
"What requirements exactly?"

The agent was a short, partly bald man in a tasteful grey
suit No tie but with a flamboyant yellow hanky in the
jacket top pocket. A departure from the slick, skinny
styled-up young operators who normally ply their trade in
real estate.
He had sought me out at a coffee shop on an early warm
day. Walked up to my little table and pulled out a chair.
"You just had an exhibition at Gallery 44."
Not used to admirers seeking my company I simply
replied.
"Oh. Yes, that was me."
"Well," he said as his coffee arrived, "I have a proposition
for you. One that you will like. Don't be afraid or

suspicious. Occasionally in life things are what they seem and are genuine."

What were those requirements? The garden was one, as I've already mentioned. The other was that I continue to work in the artistic style I am currently using and expand its horizons to connect with my heritage.
No, I did not know what any of that meant but a beautiful, big old, inner-city gentleman's residence with ample studio room, at a very modest rent, all for a bit of gardening? Of course, I said yes and signed the lease within days without giving the fine print more than a cursory glance.

The circumstances are odd but life is like that sometimes. You either live life being careful or you take what it has to offer.
I have set up two of the upper-level rooms as studios and occupied the two front rooms downstairs with my modest collection of bookcases, chairs and a table while the other has my double bed and dresser. Moving from a small flat to a large house has left room for a lot of empty space.
It is a sun-drenched day and I am looking over the physical aspects of my agreement. I need a plan.

Then there was that sigh. Repeated, through the hedge.

Should I forgo the gardening pleasures and make the acquaintance of the neighbour? A person given to some sort of woes it seemed.

"Hullo, is anybody there?"

Silence. Maybe calling through hedges is considered impolite in this area. But no.

"Oh, yes, umm, hullo. Say, you must be my new neighbour. Want to shake hands?"

His voice was in the higher registers. Perhaps a slight accent. I liked him immediately, sight unseen. That in itself worried me because I am usually wary of people. I stood for some seconds thinking over my predicament. Wary of people but having just trusted an unknown estate agent to talk me into an odd deal from an unknown benefactor. Perhaps my self-assessment needed further scrutiny.

"Not sure how we'd achieve that. This hedge looks formidable."

"Aha," he said, "Not if you know where to look. Don't move. I shall miraculously appear presently."

I stood on the top marble step and waited. There was a scrabbling noise from the direction of the hedge. Then there he was, standing triumphantly near the front gate. A smallish man, balding, perhaps fifty-five, clad in a garish waistcoat, silk shirt and striped trousers. He strode forward his hand outstretched.

"I worked out a way through some time ago. It's so nice to

have a person living next door. I hope you like interesting conversation, wine and good cheese. If you don't we can still be friends. My name is 'Arthur' but it's been 'Artie' for many years now. By coincidence, it matches my interest in art. I believe you're an artist. That's just splendid."

At this point Artie had reached the bottom step, his hand held out, a completely guileless grin on his countenance. I held back briefly, not from any concern but simply to process the flood of information from the man. Then I stepped down and shook his hand.

"I'm pleased to meet you, Artie, I'm Louis. You can call me whatever you like."

The two men held hands for a moment. Both grips were firm and reassuring.

"I'm not gay by the way," said Artie. "You're not gay are you?"

"No, my last lady-friend wanted to see the world. She left about a month ago. So far she hasn't made contact. I fear it might be over."

"I write poetry," said Artie.

Artie took up a position beside me and looked at the garden.

"Bit of work to get this baby up to scratch. A fountain would look nice in the middle. You probably should think about it some more. You know, rather than rush in and make errors."

I picked up on his hint.

"How about some wine and cheese?"

Artie looked up.

"Yeh Louis, that would be great. Can I look at your paintings?"

"Sure thing," I said. "Will you recite some of your poetry?"

"Sure thing," said Artie.

(How did he know I had to work on the garden? Intuition, talking to the agent, local gossip?)

It has been three months now. The front garden at least looks quite reasonable. The agent has been very helpful. Calling in and making suggestions and then arranging a supply of turf, a new mower and tools, fertiliser and perennials.

The owner, he tells me, periodically peers through the gate and is quite pleased with the progress. Our arrangement is rock solid.

Artie is delightful company and knows just when to be around and when to leave me in peace to paint uninterrupted.

His sighs that first morning were, he confessed, quite deliberate. It seems he is on the same deal as regards his lease and his garden. For six months he had been putting off making a start. The landlord was becoming very annoyed. There were threats that the arrangement would end, despite his poetic talents.

Once I started helping him he was quite enthusiastic and joined in the work.

"Motivation, my boy. That's all I needed. That and a strong young fella to help me. I shall write a poem about this enterprise. It will be subtle and amusing."

His poetry is surprisingly good. To my relief, it rhymes where necessary and contains a depth of feeling and character that belies the man's demeanour. I know of no rich poets so I must assume he has other means of support. It is a subject he avoids. He can talk academically all day on literature, fine arts and the world in general but not of his own background. I will not pry.

My social life is somewhat curtailed. Perhaps I'm afraid Artie will not approve. I sneak out to pubs and bars on some occasions, avoiding any chance that Artie may wish to join me.

I met up with an old art school pal one night. We both got drunk and laughed a lot.

As she dressed the next morning she looked me over.

"You know Louis, we have the same likes and dislikes, same sense of humour, know each other really well and we're great in bed together. I ask myself why we never hooked up. Then I realise, it's all of the above. Opposites attract. We'd drive each other nuts."

She was right. I could have added she was gorgeous, successful and rarely in the country but I let it lie.

My life was content. Perhaps I was cruising a little but work on my heritage and interpretations of my country were working together.

Artie had an incredible eye for good, great and mediocre so by default I tried to produce images that would pass his inspection.

Then there was the incredible phone call from Nigel Cuthbertson, the head man at Gallery Schloss the magnificent edifice near the park. Would I consider a two-week showing of my latest work in early summer? They would like me to consider a theme. Having a period or project from an upcoming indigenous star would greatly increase interest and thus sales. If I was working toward any particular goal at the moment that would be most encouraging. He would be in touch tomorrow regarding my decision.

I sat stunned for quite some time after the call. Of course, I would accept. Could I produce enough quality work in the very short timeframe? Star? Me? I felt elated and slightly ill at the same time.

Then Artie knocked gently on my studio door.

"Good time or bad time? I can come back later or not at all."

It was uncanny. I was looking over a large canvas, standing back, using that time-honoured artist's judgement call. You could work all day on a piece but it was when you stood back that you knew. It needed something extra, it was a success or it was a failure and best put aside. Sometimes I would put works aside because they had great potential but I had not yet cracked the code, the essence it required to come to life. This method had enabled me to produce several works that finally became favourites.

This time I was pleased to see Artie.

"Oh my," said Artie, stepping over the threshold. "Oh my, that's good. Do you like it because I think it's great. What do you call it?"

"Three Women at the Lake".

"What lake?"

"Oh, just a lake."

"No special lake?"

"One I know, from a long time ago."

Artie paused, as if to add a question, then didn't proceed. In silence, we admired my work. The silence needed filling.

"Nigel will love it."

As I stood, bathing in the pleasure of satisfaction and praise, a question came to mind.

"How do you know about Nigel? I haven't spoken to you today."

Artie did not look at me. He stood facing the painting, his face blank. He coughed a little. The silence was awkward. Finally, he spoke. His voice softer than usual.

"Dammit Louis, you have this annoying ability to make people around you talk too much. Say things when they should not. It's something you really need to work on."

"You're avoiding my question, Artie."

My reply was lighthearted but it brought about a change in Artie's demeanour.

He turned to look at me. His face now darker. I was quite surprised by the more business-like appearance.

"Do you have some wine? I know it's early afternoon but .... Louis .... I need to talk to you. A lot."

As I recall, our conversation went along these lines. Artie sitting forward on my old green lounge chair, holding a glass of reasonable cask red.

"I haven't been entirely honest with you. There are several reasons why you are here and I am your neighbour. Plans are afoot."

I could try to recreate the exact phrasing used but it would add little to the remarkable information imparted by my neighbour Artie that afternoon.

Where to begin? Perhaps by asking if you have ever heard of a Jewish Aboriginal?

Neither had I.

Finally, I had the story of Artie laid out before me.

As many wise men know, life is rarely a series of coincidences.

My situation and that of my neighbour were heavily intertwined. So, to begin, Artie was a quite successful importer and supplier of high-end fashion garments.

His actual name was Antoine Solal. All this time I'd been content with just Artie.

He and his late wife Delores made a great business couple and over many years quietly acquired a nice amount of wealth.

Two years ago Artie and Delores sold their business for a handsome figure and retired. They had three goals.

As lovers and supporters of the arts, one goal was to assist young talented people with whom they saw some promise.

It was, he said, where I came in.

Their second pursuit was the two large, side by side, mini-mansions they had fallen in love with many years ago. By chance they became available. They now owned both. While the buildings were sound the gardens needed attention. It seemed logical to devise a plan that would combine pursuit one with pursuit two.

Their last goal was to trace, once and for all, Artie's ancestral tree. One which he felt had many dark corners and of which he knew nothing.

For this, he employed some very expensive forensic historical investigators. The type that goes above and beyond and send their operatives out into the field, are hard to find and do not come cheap.

Artie and Delores had not been blessed with children so their quest to uncover some relatives was most important. Delores it seemed was an east-European orphan so there was a totally blank wall on that side. Only Artie's heritage showed mild promise.

It was somewhere in the story that my mind caught up. Artie and Delores owned the two buildings in which this whole melodrama was unfolding as we sat drinking our wine that afternoon. Obvious to me now.

I was being manipulated. Was it a good thing?

"My parents were a charmless couple," he said, "who seemed bitter about the world. As if they were carrying some huge burden. I was their solitary child. They gave me food and a bed. They died within a year of each other when I was nineteen. You know, despite their apparent gloomy outlook I think they really loved each other and possibly me in their odd detached way.

My father gave me one thing that I now realise was gold.

Speaking to my mother I overheard him say 'This damned French thing. We're cursed.'
It passed into my memory. Only now I see some of its meaning."

With this brief insight, Artie moved back to the story. With their wealth and suddenly some spare time they devoted a good amount of each to having Artie's ancestral tree created, examined, traced and authenticated. Imagine their delight when they were made aware of a young aboriginal artist who it appeared had connections with some of the ancestral research the pair were having done. What marvellous happenstance. They hunted me down and watched me from afar.
"You don't tick all the boxes when it comes to looking like a traditional first nation fella," Artie opined. "We thought they had it wrong. You're just another white guy. But the research was correct. Anyway we had an extra purpose."

But it was not to be. Delores died. Struck down by a wayward learner driver as she crossed the road one afternoon with some items for their lunch. A lunch they enjoyed every day in their overgrown garden.
Suddenly Artie's world was destroyed. The woman in whom he invested all his life, his love, his happiness, his every waking moment, was gone.

"Do you believe that two people can become one?" he asked me. I noticed a moistening of his eyes.

His shoulders shook.

He was torn apart. He sank into a deep melancholy.

He didn't wash or shave, or eat. Life was no longer worth the effort of living. Each day was simply a reminder of how utterly alone he was. People who knew him were worried about his health and mental stability.

As the despair carved through his wretched existence, a revelation occurred. Here he was, a hermit living alone in two giant houses, just wasting away. One morning as he struggled from a restless night's sleep, he swung his body to the side of the bed to sit upright and in doing so he felt a little dizzy. He lurched sideways, grabbing a bedside table and his actions knocked a picture frame to the floor where its glass shattered. For a moment he was horrified. Laying on the floor looking up through the shards of glass was the face of his beloved Delores. She was smiling radiantly. He could feel her love and contentment.

It was at that moment he swears he heard her voice.

"As clear as if she was standing in the room'" he said.

"Maybe it was the whack on my head but I think not. Artie, what the hell are doing? she said. Wasting your life away. We had plans, we had a dream. It was to be happy, to find the answer to a mystery and to help people. Get out of your bed, clean yourself up, put on a new suit and go finish our plans. Do this for me. I don't want you going on in this state. If you want to remember me, give my memory some purpose. Finish what we started. Love doesn't die, Artie. Love never dies."

We had to pause for a while at this point, to sip wine and recover ourselves. Artie's story was affecting me as well. I put my hand on my neighbour's shoulder.

He said, "Thanks Louis. Give me a moment. We're getting to the juicy bits."

So Delores's words imagined or perhaps not had the right effect. Artie was reborn and the young aboriginal painter was back in his sights. He could assist this young fellow while gaining knowledge of their jointly related backgrounds.

It was here that I interrupted Artie. I reached out again. Put my hand on his arm.

"My friend, 'jointly related backgrounds'? The truth is I'm not especially imbued with the deep aboriginal spirit that others have. For a start, I look more like a bloke with average suntan so that side of the equation is a little lacking and secondly I find it highly unlikely that any Jewish person could be part aboriginal. I mean, yes, you are a little swarthy but I've met Swedish people with dark complexions."

It was here that Artie looked me up and down and raised

one finger and his eyebrows.

"Aha," he said. "Aha".

It is three months later. My exhibition was very well
received. Critics said I represented a new dawn in
our people's art. Away from traditional styles into
new uncharted territory. Critics love grand, mostly
meaningless statements but I was not one to object to
their opinions. Over eighty percent sold in the first few
days.

So, now I'm sitting on the irregular once-weekly flight to
my birthplace. I'm looking down the small aisle of the
plane thinking I might ask the one cabin crew member if
they have any beer on board. There's a lot to think about.
Sitting beside me staring out the window is Artie. He is
excited. He is heading to his ancestral home apparently.
We installed those fountains in the centre of each house
garden as per Delores's wishes. They did bring the
gardens to life.
I was relieved of garden duties while I worked furiously
toward the gallery deadline. I boldly suggested to Artie
that as he was in a comfortable position vis-a-vis money,
he might employ some professional landscape gardeners
to finish the project. He did.
They carried out his instructions easily and completely.

He was both surprised and delighted by their work. He had never considered such a move. I suspect it's a Jewish thing to mistrust everybody and assume you'll be cheated. The gardens of both houses are now quite beautiful.

During this time the history of Artie, his relatives and their place in the whole world dropped in every few days as more was discovered by some researchers on the case. With each new delivery of information, the net that he had placed around us both became more and more real. These researchers were forensic. They had the means to access information that was not readily available. I began to think his take on history, aboriginal culture and two diagonally opposite bands of human existence could have possibly, touched together.

It came down to a ship. A ship that was not welcome nor wished to be seen. They were escaped felons. Thieves, misfits and other criminals. The improbabilities grew. They were French and had made off from a French Pacific penal colony. The history of this whole episode was vague, passed on by word of mouth and folklore. There were no scribes to chronicle the events and the Frenchmen were keen to stay hidden and unknown. French authorities were keen to find them but as circumstances presented themselves they saw fit to keep no record of events.

It seems the escapees had sailors in their group. They had made a considerable distance when they blundered into the massive reefs that extend down the east coast of Australia. Their ship sat on the reef for a while allowing the crew to make their way to the mainland. It was suggested that they were offloading materials from the vessel in order to lighten the ship and refloat. They set a well provisioned camp in the treeline near a beach. Here their fortune took several turns. Local aboriginals had experienced acts of savagery from the British at times when their paths had crossed. Once it was established that these new white people were not British nor particularly friendly toward the British by default, they became unknowing allies of the local tribe. Fish and kangaroo meat was supplied and a dance was performed in their honour.

A day came when the Frenchmen attempted to refloat their ship. On a particularly high tide and with an offshore wind pushing into the raised sails the ship moved.

It scraped across the reef trying to tear itself free. Success was at hand. Those on board gave a cheer as clear water was sighted ahead and the ship, at last, floated free apparently still watertight and intact. Fate is a fickle mistress. At that moment when salvation was at hand and it seemed their journey may continue, a sudden blustering change came from the south. Its brevity was such that it only gave its all for a minute or so. Such is the odd nature of tropical weather.

The ship skewed sideways. Hands rushed to alter the sails.

Swung to such a degree the ship entered the clear deep channel at some ferocity and continued to be wrestled by the wind. So much so that it hurtled toward the other side of the reef channel. A ship's length either way and it might have survived and triumphed but its hull flew straight onto a spear-like projection and was mortally wounded. The hull timbers were shattered, the ocean rushed in and within minutes the whole handsome vessel was slipping down and away into the deep still waters of the Pacific. Two of the crew nearly drowned. Like so many sailors of the time they were unable to swim. They were rescued by native helpers in dugout canoes.

Ashore that night the Frenchmen were distraught. Trapped on a harsh land so far from their home they drank rum and brandy and consoled each other with hopeless plans for their eventual salvation.

Their native friends also imbibed in the strong liquor. In fact the whole tribe found the drink quite enticing. By the time the midnight hour approached all at the camp, even women and children, were asleep in a drunken stupor.

It was not until past the hour of 10am the next day that some of the boys from the tribe wandered down the beach to the ocean's edge to dunk their faces in the water and be rid of the terrible aching in their heads, that they came running back with wonderful news.

A ship, just like the Frenchmen's ship, only much bigger, could be seen in the distance, standing off the reef. They were saved.

The Frenchmen were not as expected, overjoyed. They viewed the new arrival with horror. Carefully watching it from the treeline with their telescopes. They rushed to quell the fires in the camp and asked the natives to walk about in full view in order to give the impression of a native gathering.

It was all in vain though. The escapees two longboats sat on the shore as well as other paraphernalia from their fated ship.

In a short time boats would be launched from the French vessel watching them. Boats full of soldiers and angry officers, hell-bent on their capture.

It was at this point in shipwrecked men's panic that the aboriginal elders suggested a plan.

They would simply leave. When the bad men came ashore to capture them they would find only a deserted camp. The native's territory extended a long way inland up to the mountains of the great range. No soldiers, no matter how brave, no matter how resourceful would be able to find them there.

And so it was, with no other option, the Frenchmen hurriedly packed what supplies and items they could carry and trusting in the guidance of their new native friends they headed away through the dense, fertile rainforests of the coastal plains making their way to distant mist capped mountains.

Before they left, the aboriginal men insisted on hiding the barrels of liquor for when they returned, at some later date, as they always did.

How much of this tale is factual, is hard to say. Artie's researchers were thorough but the information was gleaned from various sources on the coast. The Ilse of Pines penal colony had been mainly used to house the 'communards' from the Paris disturbances, yet none of these escapees appeared to be part of that group. They were all newly arrived general prisoners. Deported for a whole range of crimes and misdemeanours. Many of their misdeeds so minor as to hardly cause a stir in modern-day law.

It was just verbal history handed down through generations. Such memories have a tendency to wander and be embellished.

The next part concerned and interested me. Now it was the reason I was on this plane heading for a place I had not seen since my late childhood.

(At this point I must confess that some of this story made sense. As a child I had heard pieces of it from listening to the elders. Being a child more interested in fun and silliness I took little notice.)

Faithful to their word the aboriginal men did lead the sailors inland. The journey, once they were away from the coast and thus safe, became a long and meandering trip. The tribe were not the sort of people used to white man's ideas of time and place. One day followed the next. Though in the limited, halting conversations with their hosts the Frenchmen realised these people knew the land, the seasons and where best to be at different times of the year.

They would find a pleasant creek with grassy banks and plenty of local game and simply stay, feasting, relaxing, making weapons, cleaning skins and tending to the fire. The Frenchmen noted that each time they moved on they left very little evidence of their visit. No attempts were ever made to alter or improve the facility of the camps. As nomadic people, they had no use for anything they could not carry. When the camp began to fail them in food and resources it was given up.

A sailor at one of their stops decided to add some comfort to his area. He dug into the rise above the riverbank introducing a large squared-off area. He then lined the inside with stone walls locking the rocks together with sticky clay. He gathered more stones and pounded them into the clay base of his little compound giving it a dry firm floor on which to create a bed of soft branches and leaves. He even began a pitched roof by tying a simple set of trusses together.

Another man who professed to being a cook and pastry chef had carried, at great discomfort, some pots and pans with him on their trip. He took an iron skillet this night and used it to brown kangaroo meat. He added the meat to a large saucepan together with water and some chopped yam. Into this simple dish, he placed some berries and a type of leaves that his hosts had pointed out. They gave the dish a sweet, peppery tang. The Frenchmen all enjoyed a small portion of the finished stew. The natives were interested. They weren't convinced the brew would be safe. The children were bravest and tried it first announcing that it was good tucker.

The chef was not sure he had won them over but later one woman suggested he cook his dish again.

Of the construction of a dwelling, there was less enthusiasm. They had watched the man work.

He tried to explain in some of the words he had learnt

that the structure would be here next time they called
and it would give them some shelter. Improvements
and extensions could be made every time they passed
through.
They seemed disinterested in any idea of altering the
natural way things were.

The other curiosity that took place on the journey was
the pairing of a few of the younger women with the
Frenchman of their choice.
At first wary of jealousy and conflict, the men were
reluctant to acquiesce until they found that the tribal
males were generally relaxed due to the current
oversupply of women.
Something they blamed on a dark omen they had
seen two years before. A matter which was beyond
explanation considering the limited ability of both sides to
communicate.
The frustrating, rambling trek continued with the
tribe completely relaxed and seemingly aware of their
surroundings and position despite all indications to the
contrary.
The treeline began to thin and they started to climb.
It was explained that this was the edge of their territory
and soon they would turn back. The Frenchmen were
assured that they would be safe from their pursuers.

So they reached a point on the heights of the dividing range at midday, many weeks into their journey.

Something was taking place at the front of their line. Suddenly the men leading the party stopped frozen, with their eyes fixed ahead.

A yell, a shout and they were surrounded by dark men brandishing spears. These men proceeded to scream and jump about thrusting their spears at the group. Nobody moved as the attack continued.

The Frenchmen were certain they were about to die. Then just as quickly the display stopped and the two groups greeted each other like long-lost relatives. Laughter ensued. Compliments were exchanged regarding the fearsome nature of the greeting and the suitably humble response by the visitors. They sat down and for over an hour discussions and exchanges took place between the two tribes with many glances back to the conspicuous Frenchmen.

Then came the moment that created an obscure little piece of history.

A tribal elder from their coastal friends came and sat with the Frenchmen. He had been taught some French words during their journey. Now he used them as best he could. "Les mauvais hommes viennent encore".

The 'bad men' were still coming. They had not given up. No doubt urged on by their irate French officers the unforgiving French troops were encroaching on a claimed British territory and pursuing their escaped prisoners with a degree of tenacity that none had expected. Thoughts of waiting until they had given up and then returning to the coast and eventual salvation were an option. (The natives were confident they could easily avoid the pursuers.) Perhaps they had grown tired of nursing their guests but this is all the background available.

These words completed the report to Artie except for a lengthy footnote.

1. 'No further information could be obtained in our interviews except some speculation on the part of several elders from the region. They believe that the Frenchmen must have been handed over to the mountain tribe and in their hands, they crossed over and onto the inland plains and remained as part of the quite small native contingent. It would explain the light-skinned tribe of their 'legends.'

2. The French records office was able to confirm that there were two Frenchmen of Jewish extraction among the escapees from that particular penal settlement in their South Pacific territories. The whole party of twenty-eight that escaped were officially recorded by the French

authorities as 'lost at sea'.

3. A request has been made for a complete list of the escapees with any details of their age, background, trade and other information that may be at hand. The French seem reluctant to cooperate. Possibly there are aspects of diplomacy and national pride involved. We will be in touch should we be successful.

Our plane touched down gently, revved its engines to reduce speed and then slid off onto the taxiway and began to make its way to the small airport building.

Artie turned to me, his eyes bright.

"Well, here we are. I hope you're going to thank me for this one day."

He looked at my hand.

"Where did you get a beer?"

"I know the guys in the crew."

I had told Artie that I left as a teenager to see what the big city could offer me. I wanted to paint. I felt it was my destiny, to continue the works I'd seen at our tribal place. Some warned me that the city was an angry world with much to hurt me and that I was naive and could wander off course. Now I know that they had arranged for an 'auntie' to take me in and feed me. It's a way they kept us all under surveillance, perhaps for our care and safety, perhaps as some insurance in case we became foolish and wanted to talk.

This Auntie even worked out how to apply for a grant to attend art school. She was very clever.

I did not tell Artie what I left behind apart from my parents and brothers and sisters and cousins and uncles and aunties, in order to seek my fortune. It would be up to people like Grober or Auntie Grace to decide if Artie was connected or could be trusted. Of course, he did not know that yet. I could only guide him undetected toward a meeting and a judgement.

It felt odd to be back in this town where two closely linked levels of existence continued to share life. I wondered often but never asked, how they thought the story and the place could have remained unknown. My only guess was that this place was isolated enough to have created a 'them and us' mentality, even for those few who we had not included.

They didn't like the deserters, the ones who left. It was a betrayal. Grober told me that he wished me good fortune and hoped I made a place in the wide world of art.

He also told me that I should come back if it didn't work out, adding that those who leave will always be marked. It's a trust, once broken, ever doubted.

Those that betray must be returned to the fold. For love,

protection and safekeeping. Was that a threat?

We stayed with my parents. Hugo the carpenter and Katriane the secretary.

I told them the man with me was my benefactor. It was the truth. He had arranged for the call from Nigel after all. My friend called round to see me. He met Artie. They seemed to like each other.

I took him outside after dinner to say goodbye.

"Can you do me a favour? Contact Grober and ask him to drop in as if by chance. Artie in there thinks he may have some ancestry in this place. If so, he'll be a Jewish Aboriginal."

It was here that I expected my friend to laugh, perhaps loudly.

Instead, he said, "Yeah, Grober was wondering when he'd turn up. Moorant said he would when he saw him in his audience in the city. He knew then. Been feeding our history to him through a 'research' group they set up. To get him hooked. It was known you two would meet up. It's all there brother. Like a map, like a trail."

I felt a little foolish. Of course, they would have been watching, manipulating. Should I be annoyed?

As my tribal brother stepped into his car I asked him a question.

"Phillipe, what's going on?"

He smiled and slightly shook his head.

"You've been away. Now you're back. It's happening Louis. We're all coming home. It's the time to gather. They told us, Joshua and me that we're all returning."

With that statement hanging in the air, he drove off with his casual half salute, half wave.

The fat envelope had arrived on a mine company plane in the afternoon. The pilot dropped it off on the way to his digs. Artie became quite animated. He found a kitchen knife and slit it open, withdrawing the contents as if it were a sacred document.

Scanning the pages he gave a snort of delight.

"I wanted this in printed form. Those historical people are incredible. Worth all the money I pay them. The story of the Frenchmen on Australian shores.

Well, it was all just a rumour. Scraps of an old tale passed down by word of mouth through generations. No basis in truth? Not even of interest to scholars or historians. They spent a lot of time and my money chasing up all those bits of oral history."

Artie thumbed through more of the information.

"I think a lot of what they've found came right from here. By putting all the parts together they came up with a whole. The story has substance. Seems other escapees from the French territories would aim to get to the northern coast of Australia. But in this case, we now have the people to populate the story. We can name them. Give them a life. After all the silence and denials I don't know how they got this off the French. Perhaps their people thought it was ancient history and nobody would care. Anyway, officially the party never set foot on this land."

The pages contained a single main list, then a series of other pages of names with more detail. Under each name was a paragraph of text with a brief notation about the person, their background and their crime.

It was a list of the criminals who had stolen and crewed a French navy barquentine in 1879. There were some drawings of the ship and several sketches of the men. The ship was an old supply ship and was only lightly armed. The information left no doubt as to why the French authorities were so angry.

How had they done it?

Twenty-eight men had taken the vessel at night. It was only when the drunken crew awoke on the docks the next morning did the crime become apparent.

Artie ran his finger down each page in turn.

"It will take some time to absorb all this but one thing is clear. They could steal the ship and make their getaway because six of their number were experienced seamen. Look an Aspirant, that's a Midshipman and here's a

Maitre, a Master, so two of them with all the skills. Matelot Brevete, Seaman or Sailors and even two just marked Matelot or Recruits. Good God, one was twelve and one thirteen. Probably had already been at sea for a few years. Let's see, their crimes were 'Voler des couverts en argent dans un club de gentlemen' so ' Stealing silver cutlery from a gentlemen's club' and our thirteen-year-old he 'Endommager une statue du roi'. Ah yes, 'Damaging a statue of a nobleman'. How was that a crime in those days? Perhaps the judge was a member of said nobleman's club. You know, if they'd committed crimes on their ship they'd have just been thrashed and nothing more. Unfortunately, they were ashore so the courts gave them their sentence."

He examined the papers some more.

"This one here, a Monsieur Moorant. It seems he was a quite famous illusionist. He insulted members of the Presidential family by refusing to reveal his trickery and suggesting no tricks were involved. There's possibly more to that one. What could have been his methods that would intrigue an audience to bother harassing the performer? We also have some master builders, two just called farmers, two chefs, a tailor, one marked brewer/winemaker, a blacksmith, a shipwright and even a doctor. There's more. This gets better. An Apothecarist, stonemason why even a chap marked Writer/poet/

singer/ musician/theatre man. What a rather excellent and convenient collection of people and talents. More and more of this makes sense. This wasn't a conveniently brilliant mix of trades and professions, that just happened to come together. This was master-minded and planned. They had ideas. Adds to the probabilities."

Artie continued to run his finger around the pages his hands shaking with excitement.

"One here marked as 'Escroc'. I think that means he's a conman. One that speaks four languages it says. Perhaps he was the negotiator of their group. Hah, here's our two Jews. Let's see. One was a horologist. That's a clock or watchmaker. And the other was .... a?"

Artie gave a laugh. He slapped his knee.

"Oh Louis, you'll never guess. He was an accomplished salon artist who became a brilliant forger. He cost a lot of people in Europe a lot of money. It's fate. I love this story. He has to be the link. I almost have proof right here."

"Link? What link? Between you and the forger?"

Artie looked straight at me.

"No Louis, between you and the forger. A bloodline. Murky but highly likely. Of course, there's the other bit. I thought you might have guessed."

"What 'other bit' are you suggesting?"

"Also Louis, between you and me. Our ancestors were

delightful criminals, shipmates on the ill-fated voyage to the west and ……. and Jewish. I even have the same surname. Not sure about the clocks bit. We're both descendents."

It was here that I had to put a halt to Artie's enthusiasm. "Artie, even if your story is all correct and factual. I don't feel even vaguely Jewish. I'm a native. My commitment, my obligation, my whole being is to the land and my people."

Bubbling with a frisson of excitement Artie leapt up and grabbed my shoulders. His eyes crazy with the news he had been given.

He paused, gazing ahead for some moments then added with a snort.

"All the same, I'll bet you're circumcised. Don't tell me but I'm right though aren't I?"

He paused again as his mind ticked.

"Religion?" I suggested.

"Ah yes. No, no, no. I don't give a damn about religion. A blight invented by the ignorant. Embellished over centuries with the lust for power. Judaism is just another bunch of meaningless rituals and ramblings by old men looking for something to do with their lives. If you don't know the answer you can admit your inability or you can invent answers. Religion is an example of this great fraud. Same with Catholics, Hindus, Christians, Islamics and all the other branch offices of the great white man God inventions business.

But this, this is different. This is the real thing. This isn't some made-up madness to keep the masses happy. There's something here my friend. I can feel it. Surely you feel it. It's got to be closer to you than me."

His eyes were full of a manic charm. He waited.

"Well?"

I thought back to Phillipe's remark as he departed. I looked back into Artie's eyes.

"Something is going on. That much I know. You and me, we're part of it."

Artie let go of my shoulders and held his hands up like a messiah.

"Ahah, I knew it,"

With a visit from Grober imminent, it was time to confess to Artie what I had been told. That his wonderful researchers were part of the whole scheme. Carefully planted to feed him or us, information. To reveal the story we sought.

Artie took it well. He embraced the idea. His suspicions were correct, he said. Yes, the source was an inside source but to him, it confirmed all he had heard and all he wanted to know.

This carefully hidden piece of history was to protect
those who were and are part of the ongoing conspiracy of
greatness.

Artie grabbed both my elbows. His eyes were sparkling.
"Just think Louis, we're part of this ....   this thing .... this
wondrous collection of miscreants who have achieved so
much. What tales they could tell."

Hesitating, looking about the room, Artie added, as it
happened, a most prophetic question.

"There is more I feel, another layer we are yet to learn.
What is it we do not know?"

I looked back into the eyes of my odd friend.

"That little tirade about religion. Possibly leave that out of
any conversations we have with my people. Our stuff is a
bit more from the heart."

Artie blinked, as if trying to understand my inference.
Then he started.

"No, Louis, No! First nation people don't have a religion.
None of the white man's absurd glittering gold temples
and robes and funny hats and demands of strict
obedience. No, you guys have an affinity. You're as much
a part of the land as the land is of you. Yes, you have your
stories and traditions but it ain't a religion. It's love, Louis.
Just pure love of place. At least that's the way I see it. But
I'm an outsider."

He looked at me in a childlike way. As if seeking approval

of his theory.

"I hadn't given it as much thought as you, Artie. It just happens ….. Everything you said ……. right. Still don't mention it though. Wait till our first campfire. Then you're on your own."

When Grober departed late that evening, Artie was silent for the first time in a long time. Hugo and Katriane had sat in as Grober added all the pieces of the puzzle to give Artie the whole picture he sought.

Artie had looked a little hurt when Grober explained the special abilities we had through the group. Abilities however that Artie accepted without question or query. He'd turned to me.

"You knew these things all the time while I was trying to work out the mystery?"

I shrugged.

"Not the history of how we came to be here. As Grober is saying, you're brought into the fold as an adult. That's when our past is explained in detail. I left town so I wasn't informed. I just knew how we could move around. It was a wonderful trick. Went along for the ride each time we went to the Horizon Tree. Enjoyed the places we went, the things we saw.

But the history? Kids talk. There was a vague story we shared as schoolkids. But it seemed a myth rather than a fact. What could I do when you became curious? It's not something we can share or even talk about to a stranger."

"Stranger? But I'm legitimate."

I looked at Artie and saw him for the first time.

His enthusiasm was infectious.

"I know that now." I said. "Not then. We had to be sure."

Bureau des Archives Nationales Françaises
(English)

Summary of escapees aboard French Ship 'Aquitaine'. Seized by these convicts from the French Penal Colony at Ile de Pins in an act of piracy in the year 1880.
Lost at sea with all hands.

Name	Trade	Age	Charges
1. Charles Barbeau	Midshipman	34	Theft
2. Nathanael Lenoir	Ship's Master	44	Mutiny
3. Rene Corbin	Seaman	24	Theft
4. Marc Laval	Seaman	25	Theft
5. Berle Sergeant	Seaman	22	Smuggling
6. Norris Voland	Seaman	28	Theft
7. Gilen Moorant	Illusionist	42	Insult the President
8. Blaise Marchand	Recruit (Maritime)	12	Theft
9. Marcel Proulx	Recruit (Maritime)	13	Vandalism
10. Julien Fortin	Master Builder	38	Theft
11. Emile Carpentier	Builder	25	Theft
12. Rene Gaspar	Farmer	29	Livestock Theft
13. Andre Gagneux	Farmer	28	Theft
14. Lavelle Picard	Doctor / Surgeon	36	Malpractice
15. Simeon Solal	Clockmaker	44	Theft
16. Alon Perec	Artist	39	Forger
17. Maxim Lavigne	Brewer/Winemaker	47	Theft
18. Denis Farrow	Blacksmith	35	Poaching
19. Marc Durand	Shipwright	35	Theft
20. Remy Toussaint	Non	42	Deception/Theft
21. Adrien Vachon	Apothecarist	41	Dealing in stolen goods.
22. Luis Vercher	Chef	44	Theft
23. Ruben Boulanger	Pastrycook	27	Theft
24. Josue Bonfils	Actor/Theatre	35	Bankruptcy
25. Vern Lefebre	Tailor	36	Theft
26. Tabor Alland	Cobbler	33	Brawling
27. Alon Chaston	Merchant	42	Deception
28. Marcel Lamar	Stonemason	29	Theft

GASPAR

He held the soap in his hand. Hesitant, as if in possession of a rare geological specimen.

The woman looked him over. She felt a pang of guilt. The man was old. Arthritic hands, a slight stoop, a look of eternal fatigue, of resignation perhaps.

"Mr Gaspar, I'm not sure what conditions of employment you have been accustomed to in the past but I took you on because of the three applicants, you were the oldest and thus I feel the most knowledgeable. Please understand I do not seek speed or strength but rather a wise and agreeable person to have about. As part of your employment, you have the cottage and wages. I apologise for not mentioning that I would also enjoy having you join me for a luncheon or dinner when it is convenient for you to do so. I hope you do not feel my invitation today was too much of a presumption on my part. It is your first day.”

The old man Gaspar drew in a significant breath and gave a slight smile. He stood in the elegant bathroom in front of the mirror and basin.

The lady stood in the doorway through which she had just ushered her guest and the new employee. It was an awkward moment.

Gaspar, the man in the bathroom, turned his head slightly. “That will be very nice, Ma’am. It will take me away from the fence repairs though ....”

The lady cut in.

“The fence will still be there tomorrow and the next day. Of course, work needs to be done but there is no strict timetable, no hurry. Progress with it as and when you can.”

Gaspar looked again at the gleaming white soap in his hand.

He gave a slight chuckle.

“In the field, I eat my sandwiches after dusting off my hands on my trousers. This will be a step up.”

The lady laughed, stepping forward, placing her hand on the old man’s forearm.

"How silly. I was merely replacing the soap in the
bathroom when you entered. Not thinking, I handed it to
you to use. No implications, just timing."

"Here I go then," said Gaspar, turning on the tap.

He arrived at the table a minute or so later holding up his
hands for inspection.

"They're cleaner than mine," said Tom.

Gaspar sat next to the boy.

"You're eight years old, that's my guess. Dirt is part of
your world, m'seur."

The boy beamed, looking into the old man's eyes.

The lady watched them as she placed food on the table.
A man who could engage with Tom was a rare thing
indeed.

Sun streamed in through the bay windows. The trio ate
cold chicken and salad and drank tea. A peaceful warm
day continued outside. A timeless day. Good to be alive
day.

"My husband will be back soon. He'll be keen to meet
you."

Gaspar sipped his tea.

"He's in the city you said, on business?"

"Well, business and picking up our older son Luke from
his school for the break. Luke just started at the school.
Tom will be going to the same school when he's older. It's

a rather sad country tradition to send your children away to boarding school. I don't like it but there's just nothing here on the ranges."

"I assume by the small number of cattle you have that farming is not your main vocation?"

"No, the herd is just really to keep the grass down. They have a pretty good life here with all the available feed."

"Until you send them away," Tom said, pointing with a chicken leg and frowning..

Gaspar looked at the boy and smiled.

"Mon garcon, it is the way of nature and of farming. That food in your hand once went cluck, cluck. Now it serves another purpose."

The boy stopped and looked at his chicken leg. He put it back on his plate. Paused, looked up at the old man then picked it up and continued eating.

Again the woman enjoyed the man's simple interaction with the boy.

Gaspar looked at his new employer.

"May I ask what profession you and your husband undertake?"

"Oh, we're anthropologists."

"Ah," said Gaspar, "I am impressed."

The woman sipped her wine, looking at Gaspar.

"An example for you. I note you have a slight accent and regularly drop French words into your conversation."

"Ah," said Gaspar again. My parents spoke a lot of French. So I blame them. It had something to do with our past, going back generations."

"Your past sounds interesting. Did your parents come here from France?

"No, their parents or perhaps their grandparents. I know little of it. My parents told me some quite strange stories but I forget most of them. Did your husband suggest you only employ a person with a French accent?"

Gaspar gave a little laugh to indicate the lightness of his query.

"No, not at all. We just wanted a particular person and you Mr Gaspar are that person. I hope we can be good friends and you enjoy being here."

Gaspar patted his mouth with a napkin. He took a long drink from his mug of tea.

"Well so far I find nothing disagreeable, Madame, that is for sure. I have worked most of my life outdoors. Never too long in one place. I love the fresh air and the silence and the emptiness of farm fields. If that makes sense. Now I'm no longer young I become a little afraid. My careless life may yet catch me out."

He gave a half-smile, then raised his hands.

"I must get back to that fencing in case your cattle have a mind it should be tested. Thank you for such a nice lunch and enjoyable company."

Tom touched the man's hand as he rose.

"Can I come?"

"Of course, Mon Amie. I shall put you to work immediately."

Three days later the woman caught Tom early in the morning, as he headed off to spend the day with his friend Gaspar. He held out his backpack waiting for it to be filled with exotic foodstuffs.

"No sandwiches and drinks today. Can you bring Mr Gaspar back for lunch."

When the man and the boy entered the house the woman greeted them.

Before she could speak Tom said, "Yeah we know, wash our hands."

They all laughed.

At the wash basin, Gaspar asked, "Is this a special occasion?"

Tom shrugged his bony shoulders.

"I think Mum likes you. You know, adult conversation and stuff. She says I tend to waffle."

"She has a point," said Gaspar. He dripped a few drops of cold water on the boy's head. They nudged each other.

As they walked down the hallway Gaspar could hear

voices.

"You have company."

Tom looked up at him for a second then his face brightened.

He pulled Gaspar's hand."

"My Dad and brother are back. They're early."

The pair arrived in the dining room as if ejected from a cannon. Tom ran and hugged his father and his brother. He then turned and pointed at Gaspar.

"This is Mr Gaspar. He knows so many things it's hard to keep up. I am now an expert fencer because of his fine teaching methods and patience. "

Both the man and the brother stepped forward and introduced themselves shaking Gaspar's hand. The boy Luke seemed a slightly taller version of Tom.

The man kept hold of Gaspar's hand as if afraid to let him go.

"I am so glad you're here. He emphasised 'so'.

"My vocation doesn't lie in fence building or much else around livestock. I'm willing and eager to learn though, if you can be of any help."

He paused, then added.

Most of all I'm glad because it's you. At last. Oh, we have spent so much time looking for you. And now here you are. We've so many things to talk about ...."

The man's words slipped away.

Gaspar had noticed a frown directed at the man by his wife.

He hesitated, then said "Oh. Well, that can all come later. Let's all eat. I am very hungry."

Both boys had plates of pie and vegetables and were hard at work on the food.

"I thought I'd already heard the starter's gun," Luke grinned.

For two days the boys rose early grabbed sandwiches and other food enough for three, added drinks to their backpacks and then raced off to meet Gaspar at the furthest corner of the property. No matter how fast they ran they would find the man already at work, surrounded by a group of curious cattle.

There was a problem at a corner of the largest paddock. The fence followed a quite steep slope down to a small fast-flowing creek. The property boundary was on the other side of the creek up a similar slope.

Initially, Gaspar had set about repairing or replacing the posts and wire of the section running down the slope. In the last two days, the party had waded across the creek and replaced a large rotted strainer post at the paddock corner. The boys had marvelled at the old man's ability to fell a sizeable ironbark tree with his chainsaw and drop it exactly where he wanted it. He then cut out a section for the post, stripped its bark and with just a crowbar manoeuvered it into the hole. The other end of the crowbar was used to tamp down the soil.

With further dexterity, he cut two stays, cut new notch holes in the strainer and then popped them into position braced by some flat rocks in the ground. The post was now good for many more years.

Under careful supervision he let each boy cut some small branches on the felled tree.

Their morning was gone. They worked on the creek crossing. In the heat of the day the little party were sweating and uncomfortable.

"I know a way to fix such a problem," said Gaspar at midday.

They sat on the bank of the creek with their feet in the water, feeling the cold seep up through their bodies as they ate their lunch.

The boys quietly observed that Mr Gaspar's feet were suntanned as if he did not always wear his sturdy workboots.

The sandwiches were corned beef and pickles. There was even a flask of coffee for Gaspar.

The lady had once supplied a nice cold bottle of Chablis for Gaspar. He had held it lovingly and then put it back in the rucksack.

If he had a drink in the midday sun he explained, he would

want to sleep rather than work.

"I must say," said Gaspar this day, "your place is the best place I have ever worked as far as food is concerned. I feel pampered. A very nice cottage to call home. And I have two delightful fellow travailleurs as well."
"That's because we like you and we wanted to meet you," said Luke.
"What's a travailleur?" asked Tom
Gaspar turned and looked at the boys on each side.
"A travailleur is a worker. What do you mean by wanting to meet me? Am I special in some way that escapes me?"
Luke looked a little abashed.
"I wish Mum and Dad would tell you. I thought they had. Maybe they want to be sure. All I know is they spent a lot of time looking for you."
"For the fencing?"
"No, for something else."
"History I think ... ", said Tom.
"So once this fencing is complete I will be gone."
It was as if both boys received electric shocks. They grabbed the man's arms.
"No," they cried in unison. "Never. You're family now."
Gaspar looked startled.
"Well my little garcons I have never had a family but I don't see .... "

Tom took the man's hand and looked up at him. Gaspar noted the boy's large brown eyes were slightly moist. "We've never had a Grandfather before. This is a long-term thing, sir."

Their strange conversation was halted by a figure approaching down the slope on the other side of the creek.

Once the boy's father was beside them Gaspar could point out the purpose of his work.

"Your cattle will keep escaping because this current fence across the creek will always collect debris on the barbed wire and once the water builds up it pushes the fence over. Cattle being cattle will immediately travel through the gap to see what is on the other side. It is what cattle do. Your cattle must have access to the water but if I run a series of plain wires across with barb only on the top wire and only put spreaders on each side it will form a barrier that is a lot less likely to be compromised. Debris carried by the water will more likely pass under and away."

The man looked at Gaspar.

"That is so clever. Something that would never have occurred to me. I'd have just kept trying to pull all the rubbish off the fence and put it up again."

The conversation stopped then the man spoke again.

"I'm sorry I haven't been down to help but we've been

finalising some papers and information before ….. "
Gaspar held up his hand.

"Monsieur, forgive my interruption, I am a little troubled by some odd words and flexes in conversations I have here. With you, with the boys, the lady. Is there something I am missing? Something I should know?"

The man looked shocked.

"God," he said, 'please don't be offended. We can't lose you now. I apologise if you feel any affront. It's just that we've looked for a person like you for over five years. We need to be sure. I'm certain now that there is. There's a connection you see. We may be related."

Gaspar looked at the man and the two boys standing attentively listening to the conversation.

The man held out his hands in supplication.

"It's why I came down. To ask you to dinner tonight. Roast duck I believe. We'll tell you everything. It's a story worth the telling."

They ate their meal quietly, sipped the Shiraz and used bread to mop up the delicious juices and gravy.

The silence was unusual. A portend of some event or disclosure to follow. Finally, Gaspar decided to break through the polite undercurrent.

"Madame," said Gaspar as they concluded, "that is the best meal a farmworker has ever enjoyed. I do thank you."

The lady did not look grateful. She shook her head and spoke quietly.

"You're not our farmworker Mr Gaspar. Boys clear the table, we need lots of room."

So it began.

As the evening progressed and the two anthropologists laid out more and more papers, documents, maps, historical records, old photos and even items like clay pipes and bottles, a story unfolded. It worked its way over years and generations introducing an ever-increasing array of people and places but inexorably toward a coming together of the family and the man at their table. The man Gaspar was at once, amazed, confused, intrigued even suspicious but this night was only the beginning of the complex journey in which they were all now involved.

They arrived in the town in a large four-wheel drive vehicle. Bags and other paraphernalia were unpacked and carried into their rented house. Once they were in and rooms were allocated they decided to find a place to order a meal. After which they would seek out a market for groceries.

By chance or not, they first found The Majestic Cafe.

"This is a huge place for a cafe." The man looked about as they entered. He admired the polished wooden floor, the generous tables and chairs.

"It even has a bar."

A waiter approached.

"Hullo, my name is Joseph. Welcome to my country. You people look hungry. Here's some menus. And there's some tasty specials on our blackboard over there. If you can't read it I can recite the list. Why don't you sit here by the window? You're not regulars so you must be visiting. What brought you to my town?"

The quickfire verbal barrage ending in a question caught the man off-guard.

"We're here to seek some information. Find some long-lost people and complete a story."

The moment he spoke he regretted his words. The young man Joseph he noted, was very light-skinned, aboriginal perhaps with some hint of colouring like Gaspar. His own family were less obvious he thought.

Joseph showed no sign of being interested or affected by the answer but it could be hard to tell. Being mysterious seemed to be the order of this adventure from the time they were both led to the starting post.

"Well, I wish you luck. I'm sure you'll find your answers" he said, "but first let's get you and your family fully fed and satisfied."

The food was really good. They all agreed they would be

back.

"No," said Alice at the supermarket, to the woman's enquiry about a town historical society or a museum. "Everybody knows the history, knows what happened and why. No need for something official."
The answer seemed odd.
"Oh, that's a shame. I was hoping that I could tie up some loose ends to an old puzzle."
The woman, Alice, placed the last of their purchases into a carry bag. She seemed to be considering something as she picked out their change.
She handed over the bags and asked, "What's your interest here? I might be able to help you."

When at last Alice found herself alone with no more customers in sight she made a phone call.
"You were right," she said. "I've no doubt they're genuine. Yes, I know, you did arrange for there to be a house to rent. I accept your foresight."
She laughed at the comment. Acknowledging the wisdom of her listener.
"They ate at the Cafe, she continued. "Joseph thinks the old man might be the last on his side. The others have two boys so there's lineage there. It will be a shame, I mean after all these years the Dubois and the Gaspars are

together once more and then one side runs out, just fades away. Can we interfere?"

She listened to the voice on the other end of her call. She grimaced.

"I know. I understand. If we have the ability though, it seems a shame to not use it. Perhaps it has all been part of nature for ages anyway. Predestined? Could such a small thing bring about anything other than small consequences?"

The following morning as Vivienne Dubois laid out breakfast items in the kitchen of their rental house, she noticed a man and a woman walk up the pathway to their front door. Her family were still asleep but Rene Gaspar sat at the table drinking coffee.

He looked out the window following an alert from Vivienne.

"They look respectable," he said. "I'll answer the door if you'd prefer."

When he opened the door the man standing on the landing spoke first.

"Hullo. Excuse this early visit. I'm called Grober."

The man held his hand out and indicated to his companion.

"And this is Aunty Grace. We'd like to talk to you all about some matters of mutual interest. It may take some time. We'll bring you up to date with events that concern you Mr Gaspar and the Dubois family. I'm fairly sure that our information will answer many questions for you and fill in many empty sections of your history. May we come in?"

Rene Gaspar looked the visitors over.

"Well yes, I don't see why not. This ongoing 'mystère' has left me more confused rather than less. Some answers or clarification would be nice."

Gaspar looked at the visitors once more.

"How do you know my name?"

Grober ushered Aunty Grace into the hallway. As he followed he smiled at Gaspar.

"We know all the crew of the Aquitaine, just as we know all the members of the Dharakar people. Welcome home, Rene."

Gaspar felt a strange chill pass over him. In his vague childhood as he sat at the dinner table he remembered those words being mentioned. Why and in what context he did not know.

Now, a lifetime later they appeared in his mind again, spoken by a stranger.

As they entered the kitchen, Vivienne Dubois looked up and smiled.

"I was listening. You've come to tell us, haven't you? Our search is over. Please be seated. I'll call the family and make some tea and coffee. I knew as soon as we arrived here that we'd found the place. This was where we'd reconnect. That the unknowing would end."

Aunty Grace took a seat and wriggled comfortably. She smiled back quite benignly.

"Well dear, it's more that the place found you. Was always going to happen. There's some inevitability about your arrival. Just as the others. We don't ask anymore how or why it happens. If you're expecting an explanation of our unusual world then disappointment awaits you."

Rene Gaspar stood in the doorway. Despite the talk from the Dubois family back at the farm, this whole business left him confused. That Vivienne Dubois was a relative by some marriage in France in a past century? That all the past still could exist? Yet he had no past. Was this void about to be filled?

"You've never done this before but you're sure it will be for the best? Already I am in awe and terrified."

The man Rene Gaspar and his companion Gilen Moorant stood together on a roadway. One that stretched off into distant farmlands and some forest on the hills. Dusk was settling over the landscape. Night would soon be upon them. All about them was deserted. With no light to be seen people retired to their dwellings at such times. To their left, marked by a stone pillar with the initial chiselled out, was the road into the town. A town from which Rene Gaspar had been taken following his trial for a part in the bold theft of several sheep.

Moorant spent long hours in thought before his decision. Once made he felt quite good within himself that a tiny piece of an event might be corrected for the better. They were to attempt a reconstruction of the past.
Rene Gaspar was alone in the world he occupied because following his departure for a prison in the Pacific his only son had struggled in his efforts to help his mother on their small farm, before convincing her that he could support them with an income away from the farm. He set out with youthful optimism to seek an employer.
It was not to be. Every attempt this 17-year-old farm boy made to gain a form of lucrative employment came to nothing. His lack of experience, a trade or knowledge left him ignored and unwanted. Another wandering boy with nothing to offer in a time where your knowledge and skills were your brand and all that you had for sale.
He could not face the thought of returning to his mother to tell her he had failed.

One morning the woman received a letter from her son. As she sat by her small window his words revealed to her that, after many offers that he felt were not quite right he had decided to join the French Army. While he explained, the job offers he had received were adequate, there could be no certainty of ongoing employment and stability. Thus, upon consideration, he accepted a posting with an armed unit located at the barracks in their nearby town. After a period of initial training he assured her, he would be able to make regular visits. In the meantime, he had directed that all his wages be passed onto his mother.

Rene Gaspar's wife was both relieved and saddened at this news. She had cruelly lost her husband to transportation and now her dear son was to be absent. Her life would be supplied with a small but welcome income but she would not see her boy.

At first, this new arrangement brought some token relief to the mother and the son. The boy proved a competent soldier and a regular exchange of letters gave comfort to both parties.

The world had brightened a little. Perhaps a corner had been turned.

Then there came a visit to the farmhouse by the wife of Andre Dubois, the man with whom Rene Gaspar had been accused of stealing sheep from a nearby estate. Both men were now in New Caledonia.

With her, the woman brought her daughter. The wife of Andre Dubois was in a very agitated state. Pointing at the girl's distended midriff she announced that her daughter was with child and that after much pressure she had finally admitted the father to be the son of Rene Gaspar. She demanded satisfaction. No compromise or 'arrangement' would be considered. The prospective father must immediately provide for the girl and their child and they must be married immediately to alleviate the terrible shame of the whole affair.

The wife of Rene Gaspar was in despair. She would lose her income and her son. Even if free of his army commitments it was demanded that he make his life at the Dubois farm and assist their farmwork. Despite there being two strapping sons at the property to take care of all the necessities of running the establishment at a nice profit.

Correspondence passed between all parties. The Dubois woman graciously suggested she would pay for the priest and a small supper on the wedding day, no doubt to assure the capture of a third male worker for the farm.

It was all being arranged. Simply rushed ahead. Even a brief absence from his barracks was granted to the soldier Gaspar by the senior officer so that the boy could be in attendance at his wedding.

The next Sunday in a flurry of activity the marriage took place. Guests were spirited in and out of the church before the regular Sunday service. By the time the parishioners arrived all trace of the wedding party had gone.

The new husband had to immediately return to his barracks. His minimum term of enlistment must be served out.

It was to be a week from the Tuesday that dawned on Gaspar's farm with a drizzle of rain. The woman looked out her window. She had two cows left having sold two only a few days previous.

She sat in her chair sipping herbal tea and eating some bread when she noticed a carriage stop at the farm gate. Alighting from the vehicle, a rather important-looking army officer spoke briefly to the carriage driver and then made his way across their yard to the cottage door.

A most unfortunate accident, he explained, in which her son had been an unfortunate victim. A new recruit in attempting to bring his loaded rifle round to take aim at their target setting had inadvertently discharged the weapon and the ball had struck her son, standing nearby, in the head. His death was instant.

It would no doubt be of considerable comfort to know that he would not have suffered in the slightest.

The army apologises most sincerely for this unfortunate

circumstance and would arrange for the body to be returned presently. While under no obligation, they would, as a further gesture, pay for the burial service and a small headstone.

The army offers their condolences on this solemn occasion.

At the Dubois farm, their daughter was inconsolable. She truly loved the boy from the Gaspar farm. They were in love from the day they first met as children.

Some suggested she had been talked into the relationship in order to snare the boy. So her actions were those of a body consumed by guilt.

Not so it seemed. The Dubois family were horrified at the terrible events and their part in the sadness.

Their distress would only increase.

Four days after the funeral and a visit to her husband's grave to lay a posy of wildflowers, the wife of Rene Gaspar returned to their farm, sat in her chair by the window and swallowed a draft of poison kept in the workshed for the control of rats.

It was said she died of a broken heart.

It's the way this thing works, explained Moorant. The reason this road and these surroundings seem so familiar is because you know them. Unlike others from the boat, your past stopped. You are still you. I don't know why this happens but it does. If you cannot remember a great deal about your past it's because you have lived through several lives. As we go forward with this plan it will all come back to you. Moreover, you will gain some years from the original you.

An odd payment of longevity. Strangely you will not notice and I am watching out for you.

I hope you will stay focused Rene. I'll be with you but you will be the one to explain what is going to happen. I'm quite confident that touching this little bit of your history will not cause too many ripples.

As they approached Rene Gaspar's farm in the darkness they looked about for any people who might notice them. All appeared quiet. A light shone from the parlour as they crossed the yard to the door.

"Remember," whispered Moorant. "Only a few days earlier you were taken away for transportation. Your son is home. None of the other events we discussed have taken place. Now a slightly older version of yourself is knocking on her door. It will not be easy."

"Who comes at this hour?"

The voice from within made Rene go tense. His eyes flicked about. His mouth hung ajar. All these surroundings were at once familiar. He knew them all. In his heart, his love for his wife was reborn in a moment.

He heard the sound of the floorboard that creaked, a chair shift, perhaps the tink of a knife or fork against a plate. Those thick white and blue plates that had been given at their marriage.

"I'll go, mother. Stay back. It is a neighbour or a wayfarer possibly."

His son! The boy. My God, he knew the voice, could see his face, remember his slender frame. Not quite adult but so darkly handsome.

"Say something in reply," said Moorant.

Rene looked about as if unsure. Then he spoke. In french. In his local dialect.

"Please open the door dear family. I will explain. It is Rene."

There came a gasp and a slight shriek from inside.

"No, no, how can this be."

"Be calm. It is me. I come with news."

Rene Gaspar looked at Moorant stationed behind him to his left. He returned his face to the door.

"News that will require we sit and talk for a while."

Rene heard the door latch slide back. Quite easily as it happened. He had always meant to put some lard on the bolt after it became stiff to move. Perhaps the boy had remembered to do it.

Extra candles were lit. The cork was withdrawn from a special bottle of burgundy, kept on top of the kitchen cabinet. Cheese and bread were produced.
Even in the soft dim light the wife and son of Rene were at once delighted with his presence and concerned at his appearance.
It was the man, the husband, the father. It could be no other. Yet it was not the man they knew. They remembered a younger, more robust fellow, with life in his step and a less worldly disposition. One not long departed.
This Rene was a gentle soul, perhaps burdened with worldly weariness. His eyes were full of his soul. He scared them but as he spoke they recognised the man. If all he said were true then his journey to this moment was a pilgrimage he was unaware of taking.

Only now did he rise and approach them from the other side of the table. He hugged his wife and his son in turn. They knew immediately that the man was indeed the Rene Gaspar of their memories. They would accept him and adjust their minds to what he told them. He was still after all a youngish man. They felt his strength.

The matters laid before them by their husband and father
and this other man Moorant, proposed departure from
their current life to a new and pleasant place. A series
of steps that could be taken to undo the near future and
remake it for a fairer more equitable outcome.
As decided prior to the visit the tragic events that were
currently in the months ahead, the actual nature of the
journey and the fact that they would be taken forth to a
new century was omitted from the conversation. Rene
and Moorant would attempt an explanation and outline
their new situation once they were arrived in Ville
Perdu. They prayed that the wife and son of Rene were
rational, sensible people who could accept the changed
circumstance and adapt.

Moorant had warned Rene against detailing the full
tragic consequences of events that were to unfold and to
simply extol the benefits of his proposal. Also, a step to a
different time and place would be left out as such things
were surely impossible.
Moorant sat back a little from the parlour table around
which they had gathered. He observed the Gaspar family.
The slightly superstitious nature of French country
people worked in their favour. In this age, they were more
accepting of strange unknown forces, superstitions and
magic.

Still, he was quietly aware that placing them into an environment in the future may be hard to manage.

Was he tempting fate? What consequences lay in wait? Even for Moorant, the man who handled this magic most adroitly, this action was new and its effect unknown.

There came a moment, as Moorant expected there would, where the boy paused. The Dubois girl? His love, his very hearts reason for existence. He could not leave her! What can be done?

In anticipation of this halt to the plans being made, Moorant spoke. A series of questions that sat in his mind. Hopefully to resolve the issue.

"Do you love this girl with all your heart?"

"Yes, assuredly yes," said the young man.

"Does she love you equally?"

"Yes, assuredly yes," said the young man.

"Will she come with you without question?"

He did not hesitate.

"I know she would."

"Understanding she would never see her family again?"

"Even that. Our love is complete."

Moorant closed his eyes for a second.

"Then go and fetch her. In complete silence. Make haste."

The girl returned. They explained as best they could. She

looked scared but held the boy tighter. She would travel
with him where 'er they go.

It was decided they would depart in the first light of
morning. They rested and talked all night sleeping fitfully
until past half of the remaining darkness when a sudden
urgency overcame Rene Gaspar and his family.
Much anguish presented itself as they all decided what
items could be carried in three hessian sacks. Memories,
mementos, keepsakes and some items of actual value or
use. Rene quietly discouraging the need for utensils and
tools which would be archaic and pointless in their new
environment.
As the room lightened they tried their best to make peace
with the sturdy little stone cottage that had served them
well over the years. Had seen the birth and growing
of their son and now was to be abandoned for sake of
propriety and salvation.
To a new land. One of great fortune and promise.

Moorant chose a hidden piece of ground under a giant fig
tree beside the road. He could not explain to the wife and
son and the girl how it would happen except to reassure
them that, as they walked into this area they would no
longer be there and their new destination would lay
before them. Perhaps they thought it all a ruse and that

the horse and cart for their journey would be revealed.
To his great relief as they quietly approached the tree,
there did not occur any anxious moments or sudden
reluctance to proceed.

As a measure of caution, the arrival point was a field
outside their new town. Their new life.

Initially, it would not appear odd or confronting. Rene
would walk with his family slowly into the town, giving
him a chance to expand on their exact whereabouts and
the calendar year into which they had arrived.

What trepidation was imagined and what did take place
were completely opposed.

The family of Rene were amazed, confused, delighted,
wary, awestruck and happy.

Moorant on the other hand was most wary, waiting for a
hint of possible consequences. All about him remained
untouched. The Gaspars and Dubois remained intact and
whole.

What substance would reveal itself? What unnoticed
subtle events were unfolding?

In the histories, the Dubois had uncovered, there was a
sudden emigration to Australia for what appeared to be
no particular reason.

There was also that mysterious disappearance from

their village in France. A young man, his mother and his
sweetheart, vanished overnight. Never seen again.
Their story passed into local folklore and gossip.

235

Time, it would appear, corrects itself as necessary.

THE THEATRE MAN

Benben walked along the sandy path edged with smooth rounded rocks. He liked this little private track to the house.

He took his time enjoying the silky texture of the sand under his feet. The house was a nice sunlit, sand-coloured timber construction. It was some sort of south sea island white man style of residence built up on stilts, with cool verandahs all around and lattice work sunscreens. A place where iced tea and drinks made of gin would be served in the early evenings. Moorant had claimed the crude shack that originally stood there as soon as they had come upon it, in the exploration of their latest habitat. This island of unknown origin. The place that boy Lucien had said would be safe and remain undisturbed.

So Benben took his time.

"These young fellas are good at idling." That's what Grober said once. Others then reminded him of his own idleness when younger. Benben chuckled at the memory Before he arrived his presence would be noted. It was the way.

The man was the one.

"Hullo Benben."

The voice came up inside his head.

"You have something to tell me."

Moorant was sitting on his verandah. His face was in the shadow of a palm growing close to the steps.

"He's here," Benben said. "Did you already know?"

"I felt that he was close. I can't always be sure. So, thanks for coming."

"How did you make sure he'd come?"

"Because I told him not to ..... "

As Benben reached the steps he realised that there were two of Moorants 'people' sitting quietly near his cane chair.

They smiled gently at the visitor.

No matter how often he saw them Benben was a little unnerved by their presence. It was the boy Lucien from the village and one of the acrobat's children. They seemed to be playing with some stick figures with painted faces.

"What you want me to tell them?"

Moorant was silent and unmoving, then at last he put his finger to his nose, tapped it a few times and said, "I think, give him a day or two to know our town then bring him here. Yes, tell them that."

"Grober wants to know if anybody should answer his questions. Sorta ease him into things."

The man in the chair stood and walked to the top of the stairs.

"If he's cautious. It will help. He is meant to be here of course. He doesn't yet know why."

Moorant walked down the four steps to Benben. He liked this teenager. He showed great promise as an apprentice in the Majestic's kitchens. A natural. Somehow he'd been imbued with a delightful balance of native know-how and French cuisine.

"Do you want a drink? It's a long way in and you've been running part of the way."

Benben looked at the two children on the verandah.

Moorant picked up on his concern.

"I can send them away if they bother you."

"Naw," said Benben. "Let them play. I've got to get back."

"Who drove you?"

"Alice. She got Auntie Grace to watch the shop."

"Thank Alice for me."

"Yeah, I will."

Moorant watched the boy or perhaps young man wander off down the path and then start to run. The athleticism of youth.

He moved his toes about in the sand at his feet. Closing his eyes he could feel why Benben enjoyed the sensation. His visitor would have to put his socks and shoes back on when he returned to the cafe.

Moorant stepped back up to his verandah. It was a peaceful day. Even the parrots in the trees had become silent.

The two boys had stopped playing and were watching.

"Pourquoi l'homme Benben avait-il peur de nous?" said the village boy, his head sideways, his fingers hovering near his ear. He looked concerned.

Moorant ran his hand through the boy's dark, curly hair.

"Lucien, I don't think he is afraid. He does not dislike you. He just doesn't understand everything. Unlike us, it's still a learning stage. Him being a newborn. Also, I remind you again, we speak English here."

"Pardon ..... neither do I."

"Neither do you .... ?"

"Understand."

"There's no need. You're happy aren't you?"

"Oiu ... I mean yes."

"Then why bother with too much understanding."
Moorant motioned them to continue their game. A game
he knew well. They could play their game to infinity.
He felt he had seen their future. So had Lucien.
It remained the same. It was the nature of all their lives.
Lucien looked up once more. He smiled.
"We will become friends".
"Who?"
"Benben and me."

Two days later Benben arrived in the early morning.
"I drove myself," he said proudly. "Don't know why I
learnt. Am I gonna need it?"
Moorant shrugged.
"Now if Lucien was still here he'd be able to tell you".
"Yeah, maybe I'd rather not know."
"If you want my guess then I would say yes. We will be
back you know."

Behind Benben, looking about, stood the theatre man,
tired and sweating from his walk-in. He wore a light linen
suit as if he were to appear on a black and white movie set
in Tangiers.
Moorant came down the steps of his verandah.
"Anyway Benben, we don't know for sure. Even Lucien.
It's not fixed. Just separate."

He turned to the theatre man holding out his hand.

"Hullo Josue Benfils. We need to talk. About your past and your future."

They sat under some Pandanas palms on the edge of a silver-sanded beach. A little way away some brown-skinned children were playing quietly in the shallows. Diving under the azure water with ease. Surfacing and slipping down again. Chasing one another in a half-hearted game that was more an invention for movement than any real purpose.

A girl waved to Moorant and another smaller girl turned and did the same.

"Is this real? It's the place you showed the audience on your last night?" asked the man Josue.

"Yes," said Moorant.

"Alright. I can see it, hear it and I'm sitting in it. So I must accept. You see, after all those imaginary mind games you used in my theatre I don't really trust anything that happens when you're involved."

Moorant continued to stare out across the water.

"That's a fair point I suppose. Normally people are quite awestruck by our playground then comes acceptance and then enjoyment. But you Monsieur Bonfils ... you're a man of enquiry. You want answers. And as a man who will be of influence in the next adventure I need to provide ....

what I can. So be it.”

Moorant clapped his hands.

Josue looked about hurriedly.

“See,” said Moorant. “It’s all still here.”

“Where is here? I’m pretty sure there’s no pristine tropical beach inside what appears to be an endless mountain on the edge of the Australian desert. Did I walk through some magic doorway that I failed to notice?”

“I don’t understand myself, that’s the point. How and why but we’re not in the Australian desert inside that mountain you entered. That’s still there, you’re not. There are two words my friend. The two words are ‘time’ and ‘place’.”

“What do you mean? Where are we?”

“I don’t know. I suspect this is somewhere on a South Pacific island, two hundred years ago. Uninhabited, abandoned, left behind as far as we can tell. It’s nice, wherever it is, don’t you think? We don’t necessarily choose places. They often present themselves to us at random. If we interact with them they are somehow fixed. This place is delightful. So for quite a while we’ve kept it. A welcome change, escape, a holiday for the people out of the town.”

Moorant stopped, took a deep breath and continued.

“I even had my house built here. There were the remains of a building. Quite basic. Somebody once stayed for a few years. Bits of gardens hereabout. This house was an indulgence. A homage to an old islander timber cottage with broad verandahs. A few of our people and their offspring, you know, from the town. They hauled everything in and put it together. So I could stay out of the way."

Moorant looked about his domain then continued.

"Be the gatekeeper if you will. Some of our first nation comrades set up house here. They say they prefer the simpler life but they all slip into town a fair bit to partake of the current century as well."

The theatre man squinted as he looked at the children.

"They're a little darker than the 'aboriginals' in the town."

Moorant nodded.

"They spend more time in the sun, that's all. To settle your mind regarding the light-skinned people of Ville Pedu. It's simple maths. A very small plains tribe suddenly inherits twenty-eight very white Frenchmen who become part of the tribe. Life is created and continues. Not mysterious at all."

"Unlike your theatre act?"

Moorant bowed his head and then turned and stared at his guest.

"I should clear that point with you. There was no trickery, smoke and mirrors or subterfuge in my theatre performances. Everything and everybody was real. Mostly I used people from my village back in France. In the 1800s there was or is a quite talented circus group there. There's also an Irish village I visit frequently. They have a tradition of quite beautiful singing and the use of their crafted instruments."

"You visit villages that existed two hundred years ago?"

"Ah Josue, not did exist, do exist. Time and place. Time and place. It seems these factors are malleable. Not concurrent at all. Just there. We've found time runs on and after that, it just 'is'. I suspect you will come to see this marvellous aberration as being quite beautiful once you learn to cope with the complete absurdity of its existence. As for you, in Paris, you went from one grand scheme to another in your acting and attempts at theatre ownership. It is why you came to owe many people money and why you were transported to the penal settlement on the Ile des Pins."

"That was not me. It was a relative many generations back. He died in a misadventure at sea."

Moorant smiled, he gave a little chuckle. Itched his back against the tree.

"Yes everybody is incredulous at first. It was you. Time for us is circular it seems. I don't know why. Like all of us, you just keep repeating. Variations of yourself exist. You have lived and here you are again. We are the same,

just variants of a whole. One fact we can hold onto is that
once you've indulged or been brought into the cycle even
if only briefly then you are part of it and cannot escape
it ultimately reclaiming you. We don't seek answers
anymore. Asking how and why is not an option. The
randomness defeats us. Just enjoy the marvellous show.
Periodically, for reasons that escape our understanding,
we found we have to return or more to the point move
on and the whole thing resets. In some way it just starts
over."

Josue Bonfils waved his arms about partly in frustration
and partly from this information overload.
"You woke up one day and suddenly you could do
wonderous things. Wander about in time. I am still
sceptical Mr Magician. What is it you're not telling me?"
Moorant sighed.
"I am telling you all I know. It came about quite slowly.
I am or was an illusionist after all. Just another magician
with trickery as my craft. I began to notice my illusions
were going beyond the clever use of sleight of hand.
It terrified me the first time I moved. What was this thing?
What was happening? I found myself in my village two
weeks before. I had gone backwards. It lasted perhaps an
hour. Then I was back.
I spent a period of unknowing and caution. I began to

learn the ways of working within the phenomenon.

I cannot begin to tell you how I handle this gift. Just that I do. I do not explore why or try to exploit it. Gradually you learn its secrets. Its limits. It is a craft after all. As a blacksmith learns his trade so I learnt this."

"Are you worried that this may be something you are not meant to involve yourself in? It could be a sign of ……. I don't know …… the stitches coming undone."

Moorant nodded.

"You may be right. We're simply using it. Can there be any harm in that? So far only three original people can make it work. Are there others? Will we meet others? Will we all pay a price? What I do know is that once you've used the 'facilities' you're captured or trapped. You're part of it."

"Questions just create more questions. So you've given up seeking answers?"

Moorant looked at the theatre man.

"Yes, you have it. One rule I feel holds up in my universe is that everything must be in balance. To prevent chaos I assume. Is this an imbalance?"

As the two men talked a figure came from the distance walking along the shoreline. He stopped briefly and touched hands with some of the children playing in the water. They appeared happy to see him talking excitedly about who knew what.

He was slim, tall, and darker-skinned with a quite assured, noble air. It was his purpose to meet with them it seemed. Of the first nation people he had seen Bonfils noted that this man was of a rare darker hue, though even he looked little more than the colour of a Mediterranean fisherman. He gave a gleaming white-toothed grin through his short beard. He was barefoot. Wore three-quarter blue trousers and a white shirt. The ensemble had an odd feeling of the nautical past.

Moorant waved his hand in greeting. He turned to Josue Bonfils.

"There's somebody I would like you to meet. This is where it will get really interesting."

The man they spoke to had the name Jarma. Sitting cross-legged in front of them, he settled himself, rubbed his hands together in seeming enjoyment and looking directly at Josue he told his story. Of his first meeting with these strange whitemen who spoke a different whiteman language. Tribesmen from the coastal plains passed this collection of white people onto them for protection, saying they were good people and knew many things but they were in need of safety.

It seemed a burden for his tribe and he considered refusing the request, then this man who called himself Gilen Moorant introduced himself. Immediately he knew.

They both knew. He had found another who was aware of the magic. He was not alone.

He told of how his tribe had existed for many centuries in the inland area because they could move to new hunting grounds and places of water and plenty almost at will. How they discovered the path and the way it could be done. Came to understand the mountain as the perfect place to make their crossovers or journeys. This way they could come back each time. They used the old tree as their beacon.

Moorant then retold more of his first experience of this 'magic' in his village in France as if to emphasise his reluctance to accept all that was happening to him. It constantly worried him until he realised it was a phenomena that presented no harm and much as he tried to deny its presence through logic and reason, it continued to be there at his command. He gained a reputation as a trickster by those who didn't understand. Slowly he brought others into his trust. Once they saw the truth of the matter they became disciples and worked with him.

Then came a visiting Irish musician and performer who met him and immediately connected. With Jarma and his knowledge there were now three ways in and out.

Josue Bonfils looked from one man to the other.

Moorant had insisted he remove his shoes and socks and roll up his trousers before they walked the short distance to the beach. The fine warm sand felt comforting between his toes. He was being seduced he realised, by the story, the possibility, that all they told him was true and he was part of some patchwork of existences that spanned time. That right now his feet were resting on sand two centuries ago on an uncharted island in the Pacific.

"I don't want to believe all this because it's not possible. Or is it?"

He turned to Moorant. For a moment he screwed up his face.

"Has it occurred to you that this place might be in French Polynesia close to the very people who imprisoned you?" Moorant laughed.

"Would that be ironic? Lucien says yes, it is in the area but nothing will happen. Nobody will come. I have to believe him."

"Why did you come to my theatre? Why was that performance necessary? How did you do it? Were you really in need of money? Is this trick or flex or warp or whatever, is it worldwide?"

Jarma waved his hands about.

"Ah, Ah. I can answer all that for you, sir, if I may."

He nodded to Moorant.

"First it's local. There are boundaries. It's why Ville Perdu is where it is. If you are from within the boundaries you are connected. Whether you want to be or whether you know it, you are connected and remain so. At your theatre, my friend here was calling the people home. His performers were all coming and going to and from their time as they were required on stage. Only the Irishman Aidan Quinn, Gilen Moorant and myself Jarma can do this. We have no idea why we have this ability. It was best to use a theatre that is owned by one of us. Even though he doesn't know he's one of us. And no, Moorant didn't need the money. That was just a story."

Moorant smiled.

"We know each other so well," he said.

"Calling the people home? What?"

"The audiences all came because they were our people. They would have felt compelled to do so. They enjoyed the show but they also unknowingly received a message. It was time to return. We are leaving."

The theatre man put his head in his hands.

"Oh really. Is that why I came? Because I have no idea why I'm here. I just decided to make the trip."

Jarma patted the man's hand.

"Yes, my friend. They all coming. Just like you. Don't know why but they gonna be here."

"How do you know? When it's time?"

"Intuition. That's the best explanation I have."

"Are any ever left behind?"

Moorant answered. He spread his hands.

"Not so far. This is only the third time we've needed to gather. Over one hundred years apart. But I don't think it's possible for any to be left."

"There are young people. Generations of them."

"Time doesn't stop life, love, procreation. Our numbers have grown and we have invited others, outsiders whom we trust, to join us. If you travel with time rather than remain static then you remain the same even decrease a little in age. When this all resets it will be as before but we will be somewhere else."

"Somewhere else?"

"It seems we all must periodically travel within our time. Once this has been done we can return. To the present, we have only been away a few days but it may have been months."

"Wait. What is the purpose?"

Both Moorant and Jarma smiled.

"It has happened," said Moorant."It always happens."

"What has happened?"

"We've reached the end of my knowledge. And Jarmas.

"Aidan Quinn, the Irishman thinks it may be an aberration. That it could all reset or stop. He could well be right."

"That could be awkward or distressing. If you are not in a

favourable place when it happened."

"Yes. We're not oracles, we're just along for the ride. As are you. It started and it continues. I think we've told you everything we can. Everything we understand. Why? What it all means? How is it possible? They're questions for somebody else we have yet to meet. One thing is clear. How little we humans know. There is a universe around us that we may never have a chance to touch its core."

Moorant pointed at the theatre man.

"And you're important. You were before."

"Before?"

"Yes, last time. You're good at keeping everybody informed and relaxed. You're a natural organiser. It will all come back to you, in a rush. Your whole life history. Don't be overwhelmed."

The men sat in silence for some time. On the beach, the children had run themselves to exhaustion. They now lay in a row on the sand with their feet just in the water, hardly moving.

Overhead a brightly coloured parrot called as it flew. Joined by three others they made their way out over the water then turned in a big arc and headed back into the trees nearby calling as they flew.

Finally, Josue gave a grunt. Without turning his head and continuing to look at the sparkling water he asked one more question.

"We will return then? The town will be as before?"

"Yes. If it is the same as the last gathering. We'll be back. Although we may visit many places. I can't say. Months or years hence perhaps. But we plan it so it will be the day after we left. Or near as possible. It won't be the same reality but the town will be as it was because we will have barely been gone."

"And you can't return sooner. Whatever commands our travels holds us back until a certain, indeterminate time has elapsed?"

"Another mystery."

"The future?"

Moorant shrugged.

"Not so far. Perhaps some laws unknown prevent going forward. Possibly because there is nothing there. We only move within the time we have lived."

"Could I go back to Paris and chat with my 10 year old self? Impart some wisdom?"

"You could," said Moorant. "But I wouldn't. Leave the poor lad alone. Let yourself have a happy childhood.""

Josue Bonfils sighed.

He waved his hands about his head once more in an air of frustration.

"I will ask no more questions. As I said, answers simply invite further questions. The impossibility of it all defeats me. Whatever awaits, it seems I will be among friends."

"You will," said Jarma, in his pleasant husky voice.

The trio under the tree heard voices from the track to Moorant's house.

Benben appeared with the two boys from the French village.

"We've been talking," he called. "We're going to go for a swim."

"They can't swim," said Moorant.

"I know that. Gonna teach 'em."

Moorant spoke quietly, looking at Josue.

"Before you ask. Yes, you can die. We are still somewhat mortal. Besides Lucien already knows they'll be safe."

The three men watched as Benben and the two children moved down to the water's edge. The two boys tentatively dipped their toes in the slight wash as it slid onto the beach. They looked up at Benben in excitement.

Just then the native children who'd taken to playing again further down the beach came rushing up to greet the new visitors. They all talked and gesticulated excitedly. The native children quickly understood the situation. With many words of encouragement, they dragged the two very white boys into the water. Then the girls with the gentleness of mother ducks supported them and guided them as their two students felt the warmth and joy of floating and moving through the water.

Josue Benfils watched the scene and its gentle interactions. For the first time, it occurred to him that except for the older boy, all the children were unclothed. It seemed right. The normality of this place. The tanned native kids and some translucently pale kids from an eighteenth-century French village would not be familiar with clothing used for swimming. It made sense.
The fact that he was accepting such concepts was beginning to gnaw at his appreciation of reality.
"A poet could perhaps create something quite memorable from such a scene," he opined. "In its way, this situation is rather sad."

He turned to the two other men.
"Aren't you saddened by having to say goodbye?"
Jarma looked up at the sky. He nodded.
"We're a giant family. We travel together. Nobody says goodbye. And we do return. But I know what you mean. The times and the places that must be left behind as we pass through .... yes, they hurt.
We arrive were we began, somewhat dispirited."

CORPORATE

Usually, the man in the nice car with the nice clean clothes and the quiet demeanour did not arrive each day until mid-morning.

Today he was walking across the yard, past the trucks and machinery at 7am, heading to the offices upstairs where they had airconditioning and carpet and soundproofing.

He said hello to several of the men and women, nodding in a friendly manner as he passed by their machine bunkers. Most of the work in the yard involved maintenance and repair of the mining gear and ensuring safety protocols. The man's name was Tom Bentley. He was a head office man not a local. Just him and Larry Bark his Manager. Everybody else was an employee from the town. These bosses were called the 'Twobees' because of their last names.

It made gossip easier when referring to the outsiders. Truth be told, most felt sorry for the two men. Away from their families for long periods, fighting a battle that they were not going to win while doggedly believing in their science. They could not know that their task was doomed before they started. Manipulation and local management of the 'situation' ensured they were controlled at all times.

Their company was huge. It had interests across the land and in quite a few other countries. Its sole objective was to extract ore of various forms and types from the ground and either sell it at a huge profit or carry out some post-extraction process to add to its value so that it might be sold at an even greater profit.

The company was not known for its environmental credentials. It did what needed to be done to comply with Government agencies and international agreements while seeking every loophole possible to minimise or eliminate these obligations.

In this aspect of its operation, it was generally quite successful. Nearly all its ventures were highly profitable. It did not put money into mining projects unless there was a high degree of certainty regarding returns.

With a view to the potential riches in the undocumented lands around Ville Perdu it had spent over a year hunting for a chink in the Native Title Agreement that bound up the area and its minerals for the tribe whose heritage and occupation of the area dated back beyond any hint of European interest or even knowledge of the legendary 'great south land'. The land that must exist to add balance to the world's land masses.

The mining giant's legal team found it a most unusual document. Keen minds had drafted and perfected its content with a view to sealing the area completely to any form of intrusion.

Usually, inevitably, in these documents, there would be a badly worded clause or an ambiguous definition that would allow scrutiny. Once the legal team could cast doubt on the true meaning or intention of part of a document, they could proceed to a ruling by a panel of judges/experts who would give their assessment of the words. As with most cases where the law, rather than common sense and the obvious are at stake, the law will generally win out, no matter how absurd its definition becomes.

The legal team found nothing.

So, they used the last card in their pack. The 'network'. They would simply ask for a hearing to ensure that the

Ville Perdu Agreement was still valid in this modern era.

The legal team used some favours to have three learned colleagues from within the profession appointed to the panel who would make a finding.
Almost immediately this panel found that they could not locate any person or persons who would be readily identifiable as members of the tribe to which the document was ascribed. Various persons of the town were brought forward as representatives of the tribe in question but the judges upon interviewing them took a strong racial view of the matter and suggested privately that they were far too 'white' to be acceptable as descended from the original 'custodians' of the land as it was related to in the document.
When asked for an explanation as to how this was possible that all of the town's representatives were very close to being 'white men' or 'women' and not native at all, they refrained from offering an explanation. They did howerver add a suggestion that the legal team may be venturing into very dangerous territory if they were to apply any racial bias or slurs to the investigation.

While the mining company team were sensing victory the native people asked the judges to consider the simple fact that the document already exists and has done for a long time.

It has served perfectly until now to make the whole claim clear and with obvious intention. It was therefore not the job of the defendants to prove any case or bona fides but rather the plaintiff to find fault with the document's wording. This they had not done.

Such a refined simple legal argument was disconcerting for the panel and they took some time to reassess their approach. Behind closed doors and with much secrecy they consulted with the plaintiff as to how they wished to proceed.

It was finally decided that the best chance of gaining a form of favourable outcome was to give victory to the defendants while leaving open a minor 'compromise' as part of the ruling. It was considered that any fair person would see this as a reasonable solution to the impasse and still maintain the spirit of the original title rights. Thus the ruling would pass scrutiny and be accepted. The compromise, in this case, would be that a test drilling could be conducted at one site as determined by the experts. Core samples would be examined so as to ascertain the viability of the mineral levels. This was to be a gesture of goodwill to the native people to enrich their knowledge of their titled area.

It was suggested that no such large ore deposits would be

found and thus it would be an end to the matter.

The mining company behind this whole matter had been examining the landforms, geography, geology and even the onground activity around the town for several years. They knew exactly the place they wished to conduct their vague, random sample drilling activity.
Over time now, aerial surveillance had shown there appeared to be considerable activity north of the town in an area of hills and plateaus. The local businesses already had two quite small mining operations closer to the town. It was thought that the activity further out was due to the local miners becoming excited about a rich source of ore they had discovered. Nothing had been gazetted. No plans or claims were formally produced. Just the activity as seen from the satellite coverage. Obviously they were preparing to move, unaware that their various preparations were being observed and documented.

Cleverly, it was this area that the mining giant announced they wished to examine. Under the agreed arrangement they would send in their team for one week to conduct drillings and analysis and produce a report on the mineral balance within the allowed two square kilometres they chose. Should they wish to proceed with any operations following their assessment of the site they would be granted unfettered access and complete freedom to conduct mining operations without further hindrance or any claims or actions against them.

The brief drillings and core sample reports were, as they suspected, very favourable. The site was rich. Under normal circumstances, an initial report such as they had, would be followed up with extensive deep core sampling and a thorough, detailed report on the total viability of the project.

Such was the company's desire (plus their wariness of becoming involved in a prolonged battle to get into this territory) that they made a decision to proceed immediately in the confidence that they had achieved a breakthrough and needed to consolidate.

This was, they decided, to be the small chink in Ville Perdu's armour.

Within a year the large mine was operational and producing ore from an as yet limited open cut hole in the plateau.

After some basic processing onsite the material was shipped out in giant multi-wagon trucks.

The ore quality was good, the returns were good. There were plans put in place to find a route for a rail link so as to maximise the profitability and production of the site.

Surveyors looked at the possible expansion of the as yet small footprint of the mining lease. Based on their initial exploration they extrapolated that the whole plateau and beyond was a hugely rich source.

Then the ore began to run out. Completely.

Tom Bentley and Larry Bark reached the peaceful, pleasant office area as if in lockstep. The area was quiet with no staff yet in place.

Tom put his hand on Larry's arm.

"I know it's early but I'm going to sit down and have a glass or two of a special malt whisky I've been saving for some celebration or crisis. You, my friend, are going to join me. We both need something before we hook up with the jury and executioners in their leather chairs and comfy boardroom."

Larry gave a wry smile.

"Maybe we're going to get a promotion and be transferred somewhere nice. Either way, I accept your kind offer."

The Towbees came out of the video link almost unscathed.

HQ was quietly embarrassed. In the history of the company, they had never rushed foolishly into a major project without considerable due diligence. It was the basis of all their business. Be careful, be clever, know your way, gather all the facts and make informed, sensible decisions based on facts. Know the outcomes before you move.

Not one of these basic criteria had been observed.

They were not sure if they had been deceived or merely mistaken. Either way, with new deep core sampling and some illegal searches outside their boundaries they had confirmed that the ore deposit they were working on would soon be gone and there was no more in the area. Why had they agreed to a tiny area in which to conduct their operation?

After two and a half hours there was a plan. They would close the mine.

It was to be a sleight of hand. The boardroom men were not about to let this situation simply fade away. Too much work had been undertaken in order to place their foot in the door of this strange town. Their instincts backed by a great deal of geological mapping from satellite images convinced them that the area within the title contained deposits of value.

They needed to know.

While their agreement did not allow any searching or surveying outside their now useless small holding,there was a way. It seemed an independent operator seeking to map and mark everyday geological features for a periodic updating of Government public archives was quite permissible and could not be prevented.

They would find such a man.

Once they knew they could undertake further legal work to break into the area.

In the office of Tom Bentley, the two company men sipped a little more of the malt whisky and chatted and smiled. Their futures looked promising.

Outside in the yard a lady from the company office who had arrived at work early and placed herself in a position where she knew she could hear all the conversation in the Manager's Office, now slid quietly into the seat of her car. When greeted by one of the company supervisors she called him over.

"I'm leaving now. I wasn't here."

He looked at her, tipped his safety hat and nodded.

"Of course, you weren't. You're not due in for another two hours."

"That's right," she said, and drove away, back toward the town.

THE SURVEYOR

Five kilometres outside Ville Perdu the steep hills that mark the mine sites have their symmetry broken by a large section of granite projecting quite sharply toward the road into the town. At its base is the creek that eventually skirts the town. With a range of leafy trees along its banks and a collection of nice cool swimming holes, it makes an altogether pleasant place for a young man to sit each day with his boss's good quality binoculars.

Today was not a good day. The man stood and folded up his chair. He took it and placed it into the back of one of the company pickups. He also put his cooler bag full of snacks and cold drinks into the truck.

He looked around one last time, then slowly walked to the front cab and picked up a satellite phone from the seat. When a voice answered he spoke only after letting out a long sigh.

"I got him. It's him, no mistake. He even stopped for a few minutes and looked across in this direction. Took a lot of photos. Scoped the place as if he was looking at his new home. No, no markings on the car but it's definitely him. I guess my job here is done. Yeah, I rang straight away. Okay, no swimmin' I'm comin' back now."

After the call rang off Jurum Carpentier walked to the edge of the gleaming waterhole, allowed himself one more sigh then returned to the truck climbed in and started the engine.

The phone rang.

"You did take some pictures. Please tell me you took some pictures?"

Jurum held the phone away from his face for a second and frowned at it. He returned the device to his ear.

"Good tele shots. Sharp, no camera shake. Put 'em on the wanted posters. I'm pretty damned good .... and reliable."

There was a short laugh at the other end of the phone.

"Yep. Sorry, Jurum. You're right. You are. Must have been

tough for you sitting there these last few days in the shade, by the creek. Hey, take a few minutes. Have a swim, have some food and drink. Then get back here.

After a pause Jurum replied.

"You listening real carefully. That's the sound of me turning the motor off. I'm doin' it. Think of me in that cool water in a second while you up in that hot sweaty office of yours."

There was silence then the other party hung up.

An hour later, Grober sat next to a girl at a computer screen. They were examining a series of images. About thirty shots. Mostly of a man standing next to a dark blue car. His face, his whole body, him taking photos and looking at an area where he did not realise somebody was taking photos of him.

"Jurum's pretty clever with a camera. These shots were taken from quite a distance."

Grober looked at the girl.

"He is but you're biased, Nadine."

"I don't know what you mean."

"You've been seen together."

"Damned Moorant, he knows everything."

"Not Moorant."

"Town gossips then."

Grober smiled. "I prefer, the knowledge committee."

The girl moved closer to the screen, looking at the man's head.

"I bet he's got sunglasses eyes."

"What are sunglasses eyes?"

"You know when somebody wears 'em all the time. If they take the sunglasses off they've got two pale eye sockets. They look really silly."

Nadine turned to Grober.

"You see if I'm not right."

Grober looked about the little office of the town's single policeman. He nodded at the Deputy Constable.

"Doesn't your boss wear sunglasses all the time?"

"He does."

"Have you told him about sunglasses eyes?"

"He said I'm right but with them on he has slightly more authority. Where's this surveyor going to stay?"

"I'll put the word out. He'll be staying at the Sapphire Bed & Breakfast. It'll be the only place available for visiting surveyors."

For a day after his arrival, the surveyor stayed in his room. He asked for and received meals in his room. They listened as best they could.

He was making phone calls and working on his laptop computer. He had electronic equipment and seemed to be setting it up or calibrating it.

On the second day, he came out of his room and joined the only other guest at the kitchen breakfast table where he had cereal, toast with two poached eggs and two cups of coffee.

The other guest left after just some orange juice and tea. Aunt Josephine looked at his retreating back.

"Boy's gonna starve, less he eats more than that."

It was a general comment as she busied herself at the sink but the surveyor spoke.

"I hadn't really noticed. Slim is he?"

"Could blow away in a breeze," answered Josephine.

"Say," said the surveyor, looking at the lady's back. "I have two questions. Maybe you can help. First of all where can I buy some of that mustard relish I just ate? Also, do you know of anybody with a four-wheel drive who I could use for a week to take me to a few places out of town?"

Josephine turned from the sink.

"Make the relish myself. Recipe is a secret. Been handed down through generations. So you gonna have to keep stayin' here and be extra nice to me to have your share. Yeah, I might know a few fellas with a truck and some spare time. What you up to now that you need to be driven round out there? How come you didn't bring your own truck? This is truck country here."

The man at the table downed the last of his coffee with a hurried gulp.

"Just general survey work. You know, keep the maps up to date."

Josephine smiled.

"I've seen the local Government maps. They look pretty damn accurate to me. Isn't everything done by satellites and aerial surveys now?"

The surveyor was headed out into the corridor.

"I'd be grateful if you could find me that driver."

After several phone calls from her office, Josephine was told that young Jurum from the mine would be arriving later in the morning. There was a degree of suspicion. Why would the surveyor hire a local, knowing that everything he did would be watched? Either the man was naive, or perhaps honest or he was testing to see if any areas were off limits or this was part of a power play strategy. There were a lot of possibilities. Jurum would be briefed quite heavily regarding his role and how he would handle various situations.

The next morning the man ate his breakfast, congratulated Josephine on her lovely soft, scrambled eggs and noticed he had a decent helping of the mustard relish.

"I've been a good boy then," he commented, wiping his finger across the plate, then licking the last of the relish.

"It's a day to day thing," said Josephine, "Your points

don't count to the next day."

"Wonder when my ride is going to show up?"

Josephine inclined her head to the window.

"He's been waitin' outside for some time now."

"Our people are never late," said the other boarder.

On the first day, the man asked to be driven to set points only 20 to 30 kilometres from the town. His equipment told them when to stop at each grid reference. At each location, the man spent an hour or more. He took readings, did calculations and made videos as well as still images.

He also took soil and rock samples. Even drilled down into the soil and withdrew elements from a metre below the surface. At the back of the truck, he used various chemicals and light equipment to carry out an analysis of his samples.

"You really a geologist, eh?" said Jurum. "Real scientific stuff."

"No. not at all. Quite basic work to indicate what the ground consists of in a given area. Trace elements and basic compounds."

Jurum watched, observed and made mental notes to pass on once he was back.

The surveyor seemed pleasant. He was open about his

work, or at least the mechanics of his procedures and explained what he was doing and how each step was taken. He talked of his days flying planes in Papua-New Guinea, then his work with Australian medical teams locating and mapping villages so that they could be included in the reach of the medical services. He had a family. A girl and a boy. He showed photos of his wife and children at a picnic. Mentioned that he missed them because his work took him away to remote places quite a lot.

"When you have a family," he said, "that's when you realise what life is about. When you have something you care about most deeply."

He brought good food and shared it with his driver. Jurum reminded himself to stay focused. By the third day, over lunch, they talked about the world and the weather and how good life could be.

On the fifth day, they had abruptly moved much further out.

It took hours to reach the grid points. Their general direction moved them ever closer to the horizon.

The man seemed to hurry his work. It was not as meticulous as before. He kept looking to the west like a lost pioneer.

As Jurum watched him sweat and wipe his brow, the man

seemed preoccupied. He scribbled down his notes. Took photos without care, muttered to himself, tapped vaguely on his laptop, then threw all the gear in the back and ordered quickly that they get going and move to the next site.

During their lunch break, sitting in the hot truck cab, conversation had lost its impetus. They ate and drank in silence. Jurum reminded himself that he was to observe and report, do nothing more. He looked across at his passenger, slumped, eating a sandwich, his head down, deep in thought.

The man's initial bonhomie had deserted him. Replaced by morose silence. There seemed no need to be pleasant anymore. In the still heat, the atmosphere was now tense and the young man could not understand why.

Jurum broke the rules. He stepped across the line.

"Somethin' has changed. What you not tellin' eh?"

He turned in his seat to face the surveyor. Now that he had started Jurum found it hard to stop. It came out. "Why you really here fella? Nobody believes you're just doing mapping or survey work. Anyway, planes and satellites do that stuff. You sniffing around, takin' samples, analysing, checking the ground. Seems to me you're forming a grid of mineral levels in the ground. Going to pass all this information back to some big rich mining company. Is that what's happening? Then they're goin' to get their team of nasty lawyers onto the case. Work out some ways to break the native titles to the land. Destroy the place."

Jurum paused, feeling apprehensive. The man had not moved. He was horrified at what he had said. All the instructions from the elders were pointless now. There was no going back.

"I'm right, aren't I? But why did you bring me along as a witness? You feelin' guilty?"

The surveyor did not sit up he finally just turned his head in his hands and stared at Jurum.

"Are you aboriginal?"

"Yes, I am. What you mean?"

"Just that it's hard to tell. You locals don't look the part or act the part and then there's all the French names. I've done my research but I have no idea what is going on."

"You goin' to answer my question?"

"No, I'm not, it's none of your business."

He sounded angry.

"I'm here to do a job. Simply to produce a report. What happens after that is none of my concern. I don't want to be here but now it has to be done. You were hired as a driver. If you don't like the work then you can quit."

Jurum sat for a moment taking in the response. He was not sure what he had expected. Perhaps a tearful confession. His passenger's hostility surprised him, after their good relationship up until now.

He decided to escape. Climbing out of the vehicle he walked across the ground for about fifty metres, then stopped, feeling relieved to have moved away from the situation. Standing with his back to the truck he took a deep breath and shading his eyes looked out and away across the shimmering landscape in the direction of the unseen hills. The place of the tree and their sanctuary.

It was then that he knew why he had asked the questions, confronted this stranger and his surveying. He was afraid. They were moving closer to the secret. To a point where the hills, the mountain even the tree may become visible and thus of great interest. He did not want this to happen. Whatever the man was seeking, whatever agenda was at play Jurum needed urgently to return to the town and seek help.

They talked quietly. Jurum sat to one side, his head down. His confession had not been treated with complete horror as expected. Perhaps Grober knew he would crack. The others all listened to Grober's news.

The man was called George Carmichael. He was a private, for-hire surveyor, geologist, mining engineer and

industrial chemist. A very learned chap. Well respected
for his expertise. Who had hired him was unknown
but the danger was too great for him to be allowed to
continue, especially as his interest obviously lay toward
the west. He must be working to instructions.
They could not simply move him on or leave him
confused on some distant road. For the moment he would
have to be allowed to continue.
They looked at Jurum.
He must apologise to the man in the morning and tell him
that what he was doing was none of his business and he'd
be okay to continue driving him around.
In the meantime, they would inform Moorant.

So it came to pass that at 7.30pm in the light hours of
the evening in the pretty little park in the centre of Ville
Perdu, Jurum sat with a bottle of light beer, on the timber
seat near the children's playground. He wrestled with
the wording of his planned apology to the surveyor and
with the greater question of what could be done with the
surveyor. Though this latter problem was not his to solve.
The group mentioned that Aunt Josephine had overheard
a loud, heated conversation between the surveyor and
somebody on the phone. A satellite phone that did not
allow eavesdropping. The man was not happy about the
situation.

That was all she could make out.

Jurum concluded that it was the next day after that phone call that the man's attitude and manner had changed.

"Hullo, friend. Can we share your troubles?"

Looking up Jurum had not noticed Stephen and his friend Marcel Proulx, the 'white boy' standing in front of him on the path.

"We're on holidays."

Jurum looked from one to the other.

"I haven't got any spare beers. Just this one."

"That's okay we aren't allowed to drink."

Marcel sat down next to Jurum.

"Come on, you look like you have a problem. Want to talk?"

The white boy had a kindly face.

With the motor turned off Jurum decided to wait. Perhaps the man would not come out. He was positioned so that he could see through the garden along Auntie Grace's pathway to the front door. The house like so many in the town was based on French provincial architecture. It looked cosy and welcoming.

After only a minute the door opened and the surveyor appeared carrying some of his equipment. Different to the usual bags and boxes he toted out.

He climbed into the front seat.

Jurum had to ask.

"Is that all there is today, sir."

"Hey, my name's George. C'mon, I've got some of Aunty Grace's finest cooking in the cooler bag. Going to be a good day."

As they drove out of town Jurum allowed himself a slight smile.

When they stopped he turned and said, "Is this as far as we're going today George?"

The surveyor looked at him.

"No, quite a bit further but first I want to have a talk. Clear some things up."

Jurum was about to issue his apology but the man kept talking.

"First of all, you're just a kid. No offence Jurum but you aren't a decision maker in this town. So, I'm telling you my story so that you can pass it on to the people that matter round here."

He paused briefly to clear his throat.

"You asked me some questions yesterday and I took offence. I'm sorry. You had every right to ask them and what you suggested is essentially true. I am here to assess the mineral content of this land. It's the first stage of deciding whether an area is worth further investigation. If

I say it is, then things like deep core drilling, blasting and sampling could take place. "

Jurum forgot his apology. He was disturbed by the man's candour.

"This is my native country. Nothing happens here without the approval of the native council. We are the only people who can mine here. It can't happen."

George the surveyor gave a weak smile.

"I'm not on anybody's side, mate, but I can tell you this. If my clients decide they want to move in here there's a limit to what you or your native title will be able to do. They have the power and the connections to make it happen. It's all to do with greed."

He patted Jurum on the shoulder.

"I could have brought my own truck. It's why I asked for a driver. So an aboriginal would see what was happening. When you turned up I thought my idea hadn't worked. Slowly realised that in the town of Ville Perdu the white folk and the coloured folk look pretty much the same. Except that the natives all have French names as well. Which I don't understand."

"You can change your report. Say whatever you like."

"Yeah, that's not going to happen. I've been doing this work for over thirty years. I have a solid gold reputation for accuracy and reliability. As it is I had a major argument with my client when I told them I'd hired you. They prefer everything to be done quietly.”

George laid his hands on the truck dashboard and tapped his fingers.

“When I leave here I will give them my report. It will be honest and complete. My job will be over and what happens next will have nothing further to do with me. Look, if my clients decide to move in here, your town will get lots of money, there’ll be a lot of high-paid jobs available and boom times will arrive. So it’s not all bad.”

“What will your report say? Are there minerals here?”

“Oh, it’s rich. No doubt. Major mining potential. There’s a strong magnetic flow that indicates a lot of energy under the ground.”

Jurum sat with his head lowered, his mind buzzing with the prospect of the town being taken over. Of the loss of everything.

“We have a sacred site. It’s of major importance.”

“Really. Where is it?”

“I can’t tell you that.”

The surveyor shrugged his shoulders.

“Well, it makes no difference. Those same powerful people will find a way to negate any native issues.”

He took a deep breath.

“In the meantime. I have a report to finish so start the engine, we’ll move along, get the job done, eh? Let’s go.”

Jurum sat in the park on the same seat. He had six bottles of full-strength beer.

The elders had listened to his news in silence. They had then asked a few questions to clarify some points then lapsed into silence again. After a minute they seemed to notice he was there, courteously thanked him and told him he could go.

Now he sat on the same seat in the park determined to get drunk. He had never been drunk before but this seemed the time to start.

He finished three and was reaching for the fourth, scrabbling about to extract the bottle from the cardboard carry case when he realised he was not alone. On one side sat Stepen and on the other, the 'white boy' was looking at him. His mind was fuzzy. Was this how drunk felt?

"How you do that? Sneakin' up on a bloke."

"We didn't sneak," said Stephen. You were preoccupied. Are you drunk?"

"Maybe. I don't know."

"Want to tell us why?" asked Marcel.

Jurum wasn't sure if he could divulge the details of his interaction with the surveyor. Especially the revelations as to his purpose and the likely consequences. Then it seemed most people in Ville Perdu were aware that the man was here and his two companions were hardly outsiders. They knew. They had the knowledge. He took a long drink from his fourth bottle.

Yes, his sadness was something he wanted to share.

SECURITY

Their's is a fragmented story. Generations have been
involved. It isn't a dreaming story. It is a real series
of events that crossed and twisted as the participants
tried to hold their lives together and make peace with the
oddity they had inherited.

Nobody understood what it was except that it remained
and appeared stable. They were all part of it now and it
continued to grow and entrap them with its presence.

Early in the coming together of the tribe from the plains
and the escaped Frenchmen, it was decided that this
ability they shared should be kept away from others and
retained within their ranks.

Thus began the creation of the integrated tribe that

founded Ville Perdu. Twenty-eight French males and their native wives mixed in to establish a new unique order. Time stretched their lifespans. New generations inherited memories and abilities of their parents.
They played carefully with the secrets and tested boundaries, all the while maintaining their silence. Those who were part of the clan had some key within them that kept a connection even if they moved away.

Grober mused over these facts as he sat and waited. There was nothing that he felt he could divulge without some degree of danger to their unwritten oath.
He looked at Auntie Grace sitting comfortably in a chair with extra cushions. Her office was a small homage to comfort and utility. A display of her current products hung on one of the timber walls. A large mug of black tea sat at a handy distance to her right hand. Her desk was covered in papers, mementos and trinkets. This was her domain.

Grober looked at the lady in the chair. He knew she wanted to risk some small revelation as to their situation. Her trust in fellow humans was naive or gracious.
"Not this time Grace. He won't want to hear the story, nor will he care. Our history is of no consequence to him so an impressive statement about our circumstances is not

going to change a thing. Also, he's not a person we could trust for one minute. We'd have to tell him everything and that would go two ways. One. He'd think we're all mad and go ahead anyway. Two. He'd believe enough to rush back to the city and alert the world. In this case, his bosses in the mining business would be more likely to use it to blackmail us."

The group had agreed to meet the surveyor George Carmichael at the Bullo Exports premises, home of Auntie Grace's small factory. Only those who knew would understand the origins of Bullo Exports' eclectic range of products. Items of purely decorative nature yet odd and original, handmade in a brew of native/European craftsmanship. The items sold well in exclusive, expensive city stores.
It would all end when the day came.

They had gathered an hour before the appointed time to discuss strategy.
tabor Alland from their gold mine. Marcel Lamar from their sapphire mine. Luis Vercher, chef, from the Majestic Cafe. Alice Pell owner of the Belle Supermarket. Aunty Grace from Bullo Exports and the initiate Peter Marchant from the Department of Inland Health. Still more arrived. This man Carmichael, had been in the town for weeks,

lodged at the Saphire B&B. Watched and reported on
by Aunty Josephine, the sister of Auntie Grace and her
husband Emile.

Emile Carpentier II who liked to use his native name of
Jurum, had informed the group as the surveyor made his
extensive assessment of the area. Each day brought them
closer to the Horizon Tree.

Jurum had told them of the man's honest admission of his
reason for being there, his wish to keep the local people
informed and his steadfast refusal at any compromise.
How he viewed his integrity as non-negotiable and
immovable.

The group took all factors into account as the days
progressed into weeks and their concerns grew. Moorant
was informed some days before but they had not heard
back. This gave them no insight into his thoughts on the
matter.

Now the task was reaching a critical phase. Something
had to be done.

Unlike others, this man could not just be moved on. Too
many outsiders knew he was here. People who could
make trouble.

Substantial bribes were considered. Threats were also
a possibility but quickly dismissed. It was not of their
nature to harm another human.

Hugo Allard proposed a share in the goldmine to make him part of their income stream and thus complicit and committed to their town. The flaw was that it would be too hard to have him here but not part of the circle. Aunty Grace sipped her tea and cleared her throat.

"We need something to speak to this man about, otherwise there's little point having him here at all. Speaking to us as a group might give us some understanding. Hear his views first hand but if he's as fixed on his work as young Jurum says he is, then it will all be for nothing."

"Time's getting away," mumbled Grober. "Does anybody have another thought or suggestion?"

The silence in the room said it all.

As they sat together in despondent, hunched silence a noise came from outside in the street.

Hugo stood and looked round the curtain to the garden.

"It's our man. He's early."

"Hell," said Grober.

They waited until they heard footsteps on the path and up onto the verandah then Aunty Grace called out.

"The door's open, come on in."

They heard the screen door and the front door open and close. Footsteps in the hallway then a figure appeared in the doorway. They looked in silence. Puzzled as to why the person was standing there. A boy, not a man, not the surveyor.

"Marcel? What are you doing here?"

The boy, the one they called the 'white boy', stood looking about the room. His face was hard to comprehend. He looked nervous. Normally he was a quite confident person, self-assured and friendly. This time he seemed to have lost those attributes.

"I want to talk to you all, to tell you a story," he said.

Aunty Grace smiled kindly.

"Oh darling, normally we would love to hear your story. If you wish to tell us, it must be very interesting but this is an important meeting. I'm afraid we can't spare the time right now. You see we're waiting for ...."

She stopped. Her eyes narrowed slightly. She looked at the window.

"Did you come in that car outside?"

Marcel looked at the window and nodded.

"Yes, I did. That's what my story is about. George won't be coming in just yet. Not until I've told you my story. Then you must decide what you want to do."

"I don't understand dear. How is your story related to our talking to this surveyor person? Do you know him? Do you have some information that might help us?

Grober beckoned to the boy.

"Marcel, come here. Come and sit next to me. Maybe you should tell us this story."

It was the first time ever that Grober had not called Marcel 'white boy'.

"I'd rather stand."

"Is your story likely to make me angry?"

Marcel looked at Grober with his broad shoulders and big arms. The man was frowning and rubbing his hand across his mouth. Something he did when agitated.

"I told him your real name."

"Told who?"

"Mr Carmichael, George. I told him your name was Nathaniel Lenoir and that you were a ship's master, as were your other selves. That Grober was just a name you've adopted to connect to your native side."

Grober looked about the room.

"I don't like where this is going. Why would you need to tell him that? What is its significance? What else have you told him?"

Marcel bowed his head. He seemed close to tears.

"Please. Hear my story. Let me tell you all of the story. Then judge me as you see fit."

Slowly everybody in the room nodded their agreement then sat back, their eyes on the boy in the doorway.

He cleared his throat and began.

"When I first came here, when you agreed to let me in to

show me the tree and what lay beyond .... I thought I was an outsider. Thought it was some wonderful gift you'd given me. Even Alice thought I was another invitee. Only later did Moorant explain that I am one of you, that my connection to the circle is in no doubt. I was fated to meet George and be here. It is part of the 'return'. It was always going to be so.

Once I knew I belonged, that I carried the name of the apothecary from the ship Aquitaine and that it went beyond just the name .... that is when I felt wholly part of this mystery we do not understand.

I am one of you. You cannot deny me that claim."

Marcel lifted his head and viewed his audience. They seemed accepting. Even Grober looked involved, not accusative.

"Keep going child," Aunty Grace said softly.

"About ten days ago George and I met Jurum sitting in the park in town. He looked worried. Really unhappy.

So we talked to him. He told us about the survey and how it was moving closer to the tree. About the argument, he had with George Carmichael. He didn't know what to do and he was pretty sure the elders were worried too.

He'd let his feelings overcome his judgement and now that the surveyor was aware of their concern, he may think there is some greater prize they are hiding.

For the surveyor that might be some rich mineral

deposits. Either way, the situation had become worse.

He wasn't sure if he was allowed to talk to us about these things but he wanted to tell somebody.

We tried to cheer him up. Told him that this George guy would probably see reason if we explained how sacred the area was to the people of Ville Perdu. That its message was as old as time and it went to the heart of the aboriginal existence. It was beyond sacred. And most of all, how the native title would protect everything."

"That's not entirely inaccurate," said Grober. Then he motioned for Marcel to continue.

"He seemed happier. We sat till well after dark, just talking about lots of general things.

When we went our ways it was as if all the world's problems had just been solved.

Four days ago we found Jurum in the park near the playground on the same seat. This time he had beers and he was getting drunk.

He told us what the surveyor had said. That there was no way he would not be filing a report showing the area was mineral rich with a number of mining possibilities.

While he sympathised with our position he would not deviate from his objective because he had his reputation to uphold. Nothing would persuade him otherwise.

We talked to Jurum into the night again. No matter what we said he was able to explain how it made no difference.

He continued to drink his beer and eventually fell asleep. In the end, we laid him down on the bench with his jacket under his head and left him.

I didn't sleep much that night. One thing that kept coming to the surface in my thoughts was that George Carmicheal was an honourable man.

In the morning I left the house early before anybody else woke. Jurum had mentioned that he was not going out with the surveyor this day because the man had to catch up on paperwork and his report.

I went into Aunty Josephine's garden, crept round to the side and tapped on the window of the guest room. This man drew back the curtain and looked at me. I motioned to him to open the window. I asked, "Are you George Carmichael?" He said, "Try the next window along young fella."

"I lied and said I was delivering some papers from the plane."

Grober became impatient.

"That fella was our spy. So you tapped on the next window and George Carmichael answered and then what?"

Marcel blinked and looked at Grober.

"Sorry. I looked straight at George Carmichael and said, My name was Marcel Proulx."

He said, "Another Frenchman. Now you're definitely a whitey. What a strange town this is. What do you want?"

I asked if he'd be willing to take a trip with me. There was something I wanted to show him. I told him it was a long way but his car would get there okay and once we arrived he would know what we are protecting here in Ville Perdu."

There was a gasp within the audience.
The group sat unmoving, stunned to silence. Aunty Grace was first to speak while Grober just groaned rubbing his face angrily.
"Oh child, how could you? You sacrificed the trust we all hold. To what end? How would this help? If this became public knowledge it will be the end of us all."
The lady stopped and shifted in her chair. Her arms flapped about.
"No, wait. Was Moorant away? He would have stopped this. The man would have seen nothing. Explain yourself boy. Right now."
Her voice rose.
"How could you let this happen? What are we going to do with you?"

A voice came from the hallway.
"There is nothing needs doing. To the boy or otherwise."
Moorant stepped into the light reaching out to put his hands on Marcel's shoulder.

The occupants of the room sat up in the presence of this new arrival.

Grober held out his hands and raised his eyebrows.

"You were out there all the time. Gilen, why?"

Marcel had never heard Moorant's first name used before. He looked up at the man they all admired. The man who could do wondrous things. Things they did not understand.

"You needed to hear his story. Why he did what he did. I became aware. I knew he was coming. I could have stopped them. If I had turned them back what then? We would still have a man who through no ill intent or malice would potentially reveal us. Lay us open and let the world in. Through no fault than being good at his job and focused on producing an accurate report for the people who contracted him to carry out the survey.

It occurred to me that Marcel had thought beyond our initial need for discretion and made the only possible decision. One that our wiser heads would not face.

The situation was not going to be resolved by pleas or diplomacy. We needed to change the man's mind."

In the silence, it was Alon Chaston the proprietor of the Majestic Cafe who asked the question.

"Did you?"

THE TIME

From the edge of the town it could just be seen.

A vehicle moving ever nearer, As yet indeterminate.

No more than a dark spot on a huge landscape.

A shimmering spec moving closer, yet to reach the graded roadway that came in from nowhere, from a great empty nothingness onto and past the first hints of habitation and order, then the first houses that announced civilization. Still the spec wavered about, progressing at a leisurely pace. Making its way with certainty but no haste, as if reluctant to reach the border of human advances and thus leave its wildlands host behind.

To a keen observer there would have been a slight

change of attitude, a subtle altering of the ride. No longer
bouncing and swaying, the vehicle was on the dirt road.
The tidy graded section that at least showed signs of
an improvement in progress. A slight increase in speed
ensued.
Still the machine moved as would a sightseer. As if taking
in the surroundings and memorising the view.
After a few further kilometres, would come the delightful
switch onto a smooth sealed and finished traffic-way.
Such a dramatic change.
Rolling further along surrounded by the surprising
richness of the green trees, gardens and the streets
that led up and into the centre, to the market, bar, cafe,
wholesalers and retailers, offices and buildings that
formed the small but substantial heart of the town of Ville
Perdu.
A light storm had passed overhead in the early hours
of the morning. It rained steadily for more than an hour
replenishing supplies, enriching soil and leaving the place
washed and bright. Now a gentle breeze fluttered through
the streets, nipping along pavements, round corners,
scattering occasional pieces of paper and flicking leaves
about.
Somewhere in the distance a loose shutter or doorway
could be heard butting against its frame in a lost random
way. It inferred life yet to stir, movement yet to begin.

Its noise continued as did the breeze.

If you listened closely you could hear a slight moaning.

A sound of no consequence except to give voice to the wind and its ability to create sorrowful noise as it passed through.

Several birds sat in a row on the awning of the Majestic Cafe. One by one they would fluff their feathers to dry them in the early sunlight. As needed they drank from the water left in the gutter. They chirped, fluttered, rose and then settled again in that special effect of avian nervousness.

Down at the creek under the trees some water birds called. The birds on the awning listened intently and then gave their own territorial reply.

The spec away out on the empty landscape had now reached the bitumen. It bumped up onto the roadway and then picked up speed on the more agreeable surface. Even so, its pace could only be described as reluctant.

Ville Perdu was comotosed and completely empty.

Not in a hurry to receive visitors it continued to slumber as the dark shape became less a spec and more a motor vehicle. Rolling ever onward toward the outskirts of this hamlet but perhaps now at an even slower pace, as if the occupant was holding off reaching the destination. As if achieving its goal the vehicle would enjoy less the arrival than it did the journey.

Despite its ambling, the car was now passing the outskirts of the town proper, where the people with comfortable houses, vegetable gardens and time to tend them mostly lived.

The driver gave the hint of a smile to the corners of his mouth. Could he see a little Gallic flavour to the architecture, the gardens, the trees, the layout or was he adding these elements simply because he now possessed inside information.

Perhaps it was always there if you cared to look a little deeper. Or perhaps it was not there at all and his mind was filling in perceptions as some compensation for a new understanding of what the town and its residents represented.

He would go on mulling over such thoughts for many years to come.

After a short time the vehicle entered the wide street that held the park and children's playground and then it turned left to head up the slight hill past the supermarket. It continued on round the corner until it came to the facade of the Majestic Cafe.

In a rather arrogant manoeuvre it simply moved to the

wrong side of the road and rolled to a position in front of
the cafe's main doors. There it stopped.
The birds on the awning looked down with interest on
the metal object now silent and unmoving. They looked
and looked again, turning their heads to each other as
if in some bird-like conversation as to why this machine
had arrived and why nothing further appeared to be
happening.

In full and patient time there did come a stirring from the
car. The driver's door opened and a man slid from his seat
and stood upright, resting his arm on the doorframe.
He seemed to be taking in his surroundings,
contemplating the scene as perhaps a holiday-maker
might do on the last day of their stay. He ran his hand
through his hair and rubbed his neck, continuing to
simply gaze about.
A careful observer might have noticed a slight smile on
the man's face. A look of contentment. He was at peace
with himself.
After some time of leaning on his car's door he did finally
step away and close the door. He moved his arms and
his neck, stretching and wasting time. So, reluctantly he
mounted the two steps to the landing in front of the cafe,
looked about once more then moved forward, opened the
door of the cafe and went inside.

Somehow he knew that the door would be open even at such an early hour.

Half an hour later the man took a seat by the best window in the Majestic, one with a good view of both the street and interior.
He bowed his head and sighed. If anybody had noticed him they may have thought he was in tears. It was a gesture of someone who is perhaps sad and alone.
It had not occurred to him when they explained what was taking place, that the whole town were part of this, that they would all go.
He did feel incredibly lonely.

On the table lay a big white plate with a substantial breakfast of eggs, tomato, sausages, bacon, mushrooms and fried potato. There was a rack of wholemeal toast next to the plate. Also some butter and marmalade and a milk jug. To complete the meal a whole pot of hot brewed coffee resting neatly on a thick placemat so as not to damage the table surface.
The man looked about for some time, he shook his head as if clearing his thoughts then taking up his mug of coffee he held it high and spoke in a loud voice to the large deluxe room. To the empty seats, the unattended bar, the quiet kitchen, the brass fittings, the polished wood, the

deep dark red drapes, the early sunlight sitting slantwise across the floor from the half opened door.

"Here's to you. Here's to you all. Brave men of the Aquitaine with your accidental endless quest. Also you wise owners of the land. Keepers of the story. All of you who stumbled onto the way and took the path. What a hell of a story it is. A story I can never tell. Thank you, all of you. For the knowledge, the brief time we had and most of all for your trust. I will not let you down."

The man waved his mug of milky coffee to different parts of the big room, saluting memories and faces as he did so. All there, in his mind, a recollection he would have to hold alone for the remainder of his life.

Finally he brought the mug down, took a sip and then placed it back on the table. In the silence he picked up his knife and fork and began to eat. The noise of his cutlery quite distinct.

About him the dark walls, wallpaper, heavy furniture, rich carpet and curtains, bar and grand old brass lampshades that gave the Majestic such a Parisian air, stayed mute and still.

The last customer ate his meal permanently alone.

"No point locking the doors," Phillipe had said. "Make yourself a good helping of food. We're well stocked. All nice fresh produce. Choose any seat in the house. Take your time. You can say goodbye. That would be nice for you."

He had an infectious grin. Was there something missing?

"I'll do that, thank you," George Carmichael had replied.

He added, "Why am I so sad?"

They were all there as he made his way out of the strange sanctuary. So many. Their numbers surprised him.

A whole other world that he had stumbled into.

Jurum patted his shoulder.

"You're a good man Mister George. I knew that first time I met you. This is a happy time. No sadness."

He looked about at the faces he knew and the many others who had come because it was time. He was their last contact. Once he left it would all be over, or beginning again. It depended on your point of view.

He wondered out loud if he would exist in their return. Nobody could answer. His situation was unique.

They would be gone. To various parts and places that time took them. In a day or perhaps two of their current world they would all be back. Where they each may have been and for how long was an individual thing. Some may be unchanged, others aged, others reborn or recreated or duplicated. There was nothing glorious in their journey.

George Carmichael stopped at the tree, the Horizon Tree.

The flat country stretched out below. He wondered how many had been guided by the sight of this tree in the past. Dawn was fast approaching. The giant skeletal arms of the tree stretched away up above, into the mass of stars in the southern sky.

Moorant held his arm.

"You're the only one we've ever let go, George."

"I'm not sure whether to be honoured or scared."

"Be a little of both. It will sharpen your resolve. Please remember George. You can't come back here. You'll just find a rocky dusty canyon past the tree. We can't acknowledge you. There will be nothing to see. It will be pointless."

"I think I understand. What little I understand of any of this."

George looked into the eyes of this gifted man. He gave a small laugh.

"Obviously I don't understand but then isn't that the whole point?"

Moorant had not taken the chance at being amused. He only said, "Despite my continued denials, I am not some all-knowing deity. Just a mortal man who has happened upon a small tear in whatever it is that keeps our existence and placement locked together. I can play with it and learn from it but I do not understand it. I doubt I ever will. Are we to be immortal or are we just stretching what we have? The questions are endless."

His face was blank.

He remained the enigma, the touchstone to this whole event where logic ceased.

The man, George Carmichael, the surveyor, the man who came to Ville Perdu to look for minerals now walked down the track, away from the memories he'd collected in there, past the tree. The lake, the villages, the forests, the beauty, the people, the children, the life. Those who spoke French, those who spoke the ancient language, their light-skinned offspring. All of it there, continuing from before until now. And on it seemed in a varied, random wandering.

He chose to leave. To be instead with his wife and children. At his core George Carmichael was an honourable man. He could do some good. He could spread a story of harmful radioactivity and danger in the area. Possibly it would explain a completely empty town if such explanation were even needed over one or two days. It would not hold up to scrutiny but there would be a delay. The authorities would close off the area while they looked for answers they would not find. The press would leave the place alone when it became clear that there was nothing to be found.

Briefly, he considered staying for a week or two. They would return from their wanderings tomorrow or soon and the subterfuge would not be necessary. In such thoughts lay the oddness of the phenomena. If it were longer, then their reappearance would require a certain cleverness. Though only an unforeseen event would prevent them from timing their reappearance the day after they left.

They had said they may not know him. Their travels would have faded him to a line of their history. He may not exist in the 'different' version of Ville Perdu. It had not happened but it could. They could not say because they did not know.

So much a mystery to himself and to them. They took the journeys, knew the way, accepted whatever came of it yet understood practically none of it.

There was one question he decided not to ask because he was uncertain they knew the answer. Were they cheating time or was time still in control? While they moved about within their piece of history did an account continue to add their various exploits to a ledger that would need recompense in due course.

His report would speak of impossible to reach low grade ore samples and a dangerous environment.

He would lure them away. Better prospects elsewhere.

Greed and profits would be the essence of any decisions they made so he was on quite safe ground. The mountains and that tree would never be touched.

After what would seem a minor disappearance these travellers would reinstate their little island paradise because they liked it and Moorant and the others who stayed by the tree and crossover point preferred some continuity. A piece of normality in their abnormal state.

He thought again of his farewell from the mountain. When finally at the bottom of the track the man made his way out onto the plains, walking toward his car. At a point away from the cliffs where he could make out the tree and the rock platform beside it, he turned. High above and away, were they still there, watching?

He stood for a time just looking, somehow wanting it to be a fixed scene that he could conjure up at points in the rest of his life when he wanted to see it once more.

He recalled of the final words of Gilen Moorant. They had walked together a little further down the track away from the tree, away from the crowd, to a rock outcrop that formed a small walled lookout. Moorant leaned on the rock edge and gazed across the vast plain below.

"So, the moment of goodbye," said George Carmichael.

"Yes," replied Moorant.

The Illusionist was distracted. He seemed in a reflective mood. In the silence of the early dawn light he finally spoke, softly, as if he was unburdening himself.

"I look at the dictators and despots, lords of industry, the champions and the heroes, all those religious masters, the famous and infamous, all the giant egos of humanity as they come and they go .... then I look up at the universe."

He paused and glanced sideways at George.

"How incredibly tiny we are."

George Carmichael, the only man they'd ever let go, now alone on the plain, had dropped his head.

It was over.

Then as a final dramatic act he lifted his face to the tree once more, removed his hat and took a deep sincere bow. He hoped they'd seen him and appreciated the gesture.

Placing his hat back on his head he moved off, walked to his car in the first long strong rays of sunlight, ready for the journey back, to the town and beyond.

George Carmichael left Ville Perdu later that morning. He took his time travelling through the town until he reached the long straight road that would take him eventaully to the intersection at Revensburg.

He accelerated his vehicle realising the considerable distance he had to travel.

For some time the man was barely aware of his surroundings. On a completely empty road he simply rolled along deep in thought, recalling events of the last weeks.

What a story, he could never tell. Things that he barely believed or could comprehend. Now he must put it all behind him and get on with living his life. It was a chapter and it was closed. He would not, could not, return.

It was at this point, a fair way into his journey that his car swerved and then corrected and eventually pulled to the side of the road and stopped.

George Carmichael turned off the motor and sat staring blankly out of his car window. In the back of his mind he was recalling a partly heard conversation from inside the mountain as the people poured in ready to start their journey. Their departure and return.

Somebody behind him had been talking to a companion. It had come to the surveyor's head and mixed with all the other conversation going on about him. Now it stood out in his mind silent and alone.

"Once you've been in, once you step through, it has you, you're now part of it."

www.ingramcontent.com/pod-product-compliance
Lightning Source LLC
Chambersburg PA
CBHW071131180726
48291CB00007B/2134